"You are determined not to mellow an inch, are you not?"

Andreas continued. "I am cast into the role of wicked philanderer, making it easier for you to ignore the truth," he stated flatly.

"The truth?" Sophy asked warily, wondering what was coming.

"The truth your body recognized from the first moment we met, that we are compatible sexually in a way that happens with few couples." He looked at her, daring her to deny it.

"We're not a couple," she pointed out swiftly, hot color burning her cheeks, "and you can't possibly say that considering we've never even—slept together."

"I am more than willing to put my theory to the test," Andreas offered helpfully.

GREEK TYCOONS

**They're the men who have everything—
except a bride...**

Wealth, power, charm—what else could a
heart-stoppingly handsome tycoon need?
In the GREEK TYCOONS miniseries you
have already been introduced to some
gorgeous Greek multimillionaires who are
in need of wives.

Now it's the turn of favorite
Presents® author **Helen Brooks**,
with her attention-grabbing romance
THE GREEK TYCOON'S BRIDE

This tycoon has met his match, and he's
decided he *has* to have her...*whatever* that takes!

Helen Brooks

THE GREEK TYCOON'S BRIDE

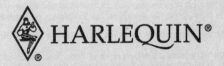

TORONTO • NEW YORK • LONDON
AMSTERDAM • PARIS • SYDNEY • HAMBURG
STOCKHOLM • ATHENS • TOKYO • MILAN • MADRID
PRAGUE • WARSAW • BUDAPEST • AUCKLAND

ISBN 0-373-12255-1

THE GREEK TYCOON'S BRIDE

First North American Publication 2002.

CHAPTER ONE

'YOU'RE not seriously telling me you're actually considering going to Greece, Jill? You can't, you just can't.' Sophy tried very hard not to glare as she looked at the small, slim girl sitting opposite her but it was hard. 'You don't owe Theodore's family a thing and you know it. Michael is seven years old now and they have never so much as acknowledged his existence.'

'Well, they didn't know about it for the first couple of years,' Jill said reasonably.

'And when they found out? You'd have expected some sort of contact—a letter, a phone call, *something*.'

'According to Christos, the family did try to write but they never received an answer to any of their letters.'

'And you believe that?' Sophy's voice was scornful, her violet-blue eyes expressing her opinion of Jill's in-laws as forcefully as her voice.

'It *is* possible, Sophy.' Jill gazed miserably at her twin, her own violet-blue eyes dark and tragic and her face very white. 'Theodore was a very proud man, excessively so—you know that. He said he would never forgive them and he meant it. He…he could be implacable when he made up his mind about anything.'

'But he would have talked to you about it,' Sophy pressed urgently. 'At least to tell you he'd received some correspondence?'

'No.' Jill turned away, busying herself folding some washing she had just brought indoors. 'Not necessarily, not if he'd already made up his mind. When we got married he told me I was his family from that point on and that he had no other, and he meant it. I wasn't allowed to even discuss them, if you want to know the truth.'

Sophy stared at her sister's bent head and not for the first time wondered how happy Jill's marriage had really been. But that was irrelevant now anyway. Six weeks ago Theodore had been killed in a freak accident when the car he had been driving had been crushed by a falling tree at the height of a bad storm.

With that in mind, Sophy now said gently, 'But the funeral, Jill? They never even came to Theodore's funeral.'

'Christos told them it had been Theodore's wishes.' And at Sophy's loud snort of disbelief, Jill raised her blonde head and looked straight at her sister. 'It was true, Sophy. There were letters which Theodore had placed in Christos's safe-keeping some years ago. I didn't even know anything about them until Theodore died and then Christos felt he ought to tell me before he sent them to Greece. I think he suspected what they contained.'

'Letters?' Sophy took a quick gulp of coffee as she watched Jill continue to fold the washing in the big wicker laundry basket on the kitchen table. 'Letters to whom, exactly?'

'To his family. In…in the event of his illness or death. Of course he didn't expect it would happen so soon or suddenly—' Jill stopped abruptly, taking a deep breath before she continued, 'Anyway, Christos and I made the decision to open the letters and read them before we sent them, the day after the accident, and then…then we destroyed them. But Christos felt he had to phone the family and just say Theodore had left instructions he didn't want them there.'

Jill now stopped speaking, laying her head on the edge of the laundry basket in front of her and bursting into tears. Sophy jumped to her feet, rushing to her twin's side and putting her arm round Jill's shaking shoulders as she said urgently, 'Oh, love, what is it? Come on, everything will be all right.'

'They were awful, Sophy.' As Jill raised streaming eyes, she was choking on the sobs she was trying to stifle. 'Really awful. So bitter and hard and cold. I…I couldn't send them. Not to his mother and everyone. Think how they'd feel after what has happened to Theodore. So—' she reached into the laundry basket and extracted a newly dried handkerchief from the pile of sweet-smelling washing '—so I burnt them. I burnt them all. Do you think that was wrong of me?'

She raised haunted eyes to her sister's face and Sophy stared at her, her blue eyes reflecting her concern for her beloved twin. 'Of course not,' she said softly, smoothing back a lock of fine, ash-blonde hair from Jill's brow. 'What good would it do to just perpetuate all the misery? Heartache breeds heartache.'

'That's what I thought.' Jill dabbed at her eyes as she said, 'Christos said the decision had to be mine and mine alone, and once I'd made it he said he agreed with me, but it's been like a lead weight round my heart ever since. Theodore gave those letters to Christos, believing Christos would do what he wanted, and I…I burnt them. He would never forgive me if he knew.'

It seemed to her that Jill's husband had majored in unforgiveness, Sophy thought grimly. She had always had reservations about Theodore and the two of them had never hit it off, something Sophy knew Jill had sensed from the first time she had introduced them. Consequently Jill had been guarded in anything she said about Theodore and for the first time the two girls had had an area in their lives in which they were less than totally frank with each other, although neither of them had acknowledged it.

It had been less of a problem than it might have been, owing to the fact that within three months of Jill meeting

Theodore—just after the two girls had finished university— Sophy had been offered a wonderful opportunity on the strength of her degree in Maths and Business Studies to work in London as a trainee buyer for one of the top fashion companies.

She had left Cambridge—her home town—within the month, just days before Jill had discovered she was pregnant with Michael, necessitating a hasty register office wedding which Sophy had attended before shooting off back to the capital. From that point the twins' lives had gone in very different directions—Jill looking after her family and helping her husband in his very successful restaurant business, of which Christos was a partner, and Sophy following her own star in her dream career and rising to her present position of fashion buyer.

Sophy had always held the private opinion that Theodore had got her sister pregnant purposely, knowing Jill was unable to take the Pill due to being the one woman in several hundred thousand it made ill—but she had been wise enough to keep her suspicions to herself. However, over the years she had seen her sister change from the bright, sparkling, happy creature of former days to a mere shadow of the old Jill: quiet, withdrawn and totally under her dominant husband's control. But Jill had never complained and had always changed the subject when Sophy had tried to ascertain if all was well, and so she had had to leave the matter of Jill's marriage alone and respect her twin's privacy.

'So...' Sophy brought their attention back to the letter lying at the side of the laundry basket which had started their discussion in the first place. 'You feel you ought to go and meet Theodore's family, then.' She could understand her sister's decision a little better in view of what had transpired, although it still felt like allowing a lamb to walk into the wolf's den.

'Just for a short holiday, like they've suggested. They can meet Michael and, more importantly, Michael can meet them and get to know the only grandparents he has.' The twins' father had walked out just after they were born and their mother had died some years ago.

'And then?' Sophy asked gently.

'Then we'll come back and carry on like before,' Jill said quietly. 'I can help Christos in the business; we've already talked about that, and Michael can carry on at his present school with all his friends. I wouldn't even think about staying out there, Sophy, if that's what you're worried about.'

She didn't know what she was worried about exactly, except that if the family were anything at all like Theodore they would persuade her easy-going sister that black was white. Jill had always been the malleable, docile one, acquiescent to a fault and utterly unable to stand up for herself.

'Look, if you're uneasy about me going alone with Michael, why don't you come too?' Jill said matter-of-factly. 'Theodore's father has already offered to pay for me and Michael and a friend—his suggestion, Sophy. He wrote I might feel more comfortable if I brought a friend along too. I'd much prefer you to come with me but I thought you'd probably be too busy. I know you've been backwards and forwards to Paris like a boomerang the last few weeks and I didn't want to add to your stress levels!'

'That's all finished now the collections are reviewed,' Sophy said thoughtfully. 'The next few weeks will be more low-key, besides which I've still got some holiday left from last year, let alone this! When are you thinking of going?'

'Any time. I'll fit in with you,' Jill said quickly. 'Do you think you could come, then? Oh, Sophy, it'd make all the difference!' And she burst into tears again which immediately settled the issue as far as Sophy was concerned, without another word being said.

Jill needed her. The job, work commitments and anything else came a very poor second to that.

The Greek airport was typical of all airports, crowded and noisy and confusing, but the journey had been relatively comfortable and Michael's excited chatter had kept both women occupied and taken their minds off the forthcoming meeting with Theodore's estranged family. Sophy had been busy with making sure their luggage was intact and that Michael didn't disappear for the last few minutes—Jill being in something of a daze—and so she only became aware of the tall dark man waiting for them when Jill gripped her arm and breathed, 'Sophy, that's Andreas, Theodore's brother—it has to be. Look how he's watching us.'

She turned to look in the direction in which her sister was staring, keeping one hand on Michael who was jumping about like a small jack-in-the-box, and then became transfixed herself as her eyes met the hard, black, narrowed gaze riveted on the women.

There was no time to make any comment because in the next instant the man was making his way towards them, his tall, lean powerful body cutting through the crowd as though it didn't exist.

'Mrs Karydis? Jill Karydis?' His voice was deep and gravelly and strongly accented, and dark eyes flashed from one twin to the other, eyes that were set in a face that was cold and handsome.

Jill seemed to have gone into some sort of frozen limbo, and after waiting a second Sophy was forced to say, 'This is Jill,' as she indicated the pale silent figure at her side, 'and Michael too of course,' as she brought her small nephew in front of her. 'How do you do, Mr…?'

'Please call me Andreas.'

As soon as she had spoken, he had transferred his attention to Jill, who was gripping Sophy's arm as though her life depended on it, and still didn't seem able to speak. And then, as he held out his hand, Jill seemed to come to life—much to Sophy's relief—saying, 'Hello, Andreas,' as she let go of her sister's arm. 'Thank you so much for coming to meet us.'

'It is a pleasure,' Theodore's brother said coolly.

Sophy could well understand Jill's present state of shock because she was feeling a bit that way herself. The man in front of them was nothing like Theodore—which was a relief in one way. Theodore had been just a little taller than Jill, his light brown hair and brown eyes pleasant but unremarkable, and his body stocky if anything.

His brother was aggressively handsome, at least six foot tall, with a powerful top-heavy masculinity that didn't detract from the lean muscled body's impact on the senses. His eyes were not dark brown, as she had thought, but a deep compelling grey, and his hair was black—jet-black.

But there was one area in which Andreas's resemblance to his brother was evident: there was no sign of softness about him at all. He could have been fashioned from a slab of granite.

And then Sophy had to recant the last thought as the grey eyes fastened on Michael's inquiring young face, and, letting go of his sister-in-law's hand, Andreas knelt down in front of his young nephew and said softly, 'Manchester United, eh?' He nodded gently at Michael's tee-shirt—his favourite, which Sophy had bought her nephew for his last birthday—as he said, 'I, too, am a fan of the football. We will have to have a kick around together, yes? You would like this, Michael?

'*Yes.*' It was said with great fervency. And then Michael added, his voice quieter, 'You're my daddy's brother, aren't you?'

Andreas didn't move and his face didn't change as he said softly, 'Yes, Michael, I am your daddy's brother, which makes me your uncle. This is good, eh? This means that already we are friends?'

Brown eyes, very like Theodore's, stared into grey, and for a long moment Michael surveyed his new uncle. And then, coming to a decision which was self-evident, he smiled sunnily and nodded.

Andreas ruffled the boy's hair before standing again, and Sophy was glad of the extra moment or two. This big, virile male was a little daunting, to say the least. Before he had spoken to Michael, she would have said he didn't seem quite human, but then the complete metamorphosis had thrown her even more.

And then Andreas was looking directly at her, his grey eyes smoky dark and almost black, and his voice was smooth and expressionless as he said, 'And this must be Sophy, yes? Jill's letter did not prepare us for the event of there being two of her; she said merely that her sister would be accompanying her.'

Sophy stiffened immediately. She and Jill had been devoted to each other from tiny children, but both girls had always fought for their individuality from those around them, recognising that the fact that they were identical was a mixed blessing.

Some people automatically assumed that because they looked so uncannily alike they functioned with one brain and one voice. The truth of the matter was that they were dissimilar in temperament and behaviour. In fact, they were almost direct opposites.

'How do you do, Andreas?' Sophy said politely, but with a certain edge to her voice which was not lost on the dark man watching her so intently. 'I'm Jill's twin, as I'm sure you've guessed.' She forced a cool smile and hoped he'd take the hint.

Andreas nodded, his gaze going over her steadily as though he was endeavouring to read what she was thinking. 'I am pleased to meet you, Sophy,' he said evenly, before turning again to Jill with an abruptness which made Sophy feel she had been cursorily dismissed. She blinked, staring at the cold male profile with a feeling of dislike as she heard Andreas say, 'The car is waiting outside, if you are ready, and I know my parents are anxious to welcome you into their home. Shall we go?'

'Yes, of course. Thank you,' Jill said quickly.

Andreas had summoned a porter with an inclination of his head as he had been speaking and Jill's quiet voice fell into an empty void as he spoke to the young man in rapid Greek.

Jill looked, and had sounded, utterly bemused, and as Sophy watched her sister smooth her straight silky fringe with nervous fingers, she frowned to herself. Jill was supposed to be coming here to relax and meet Theodore's family in a spirit of reconciliation, and in Sophy's opinion the Karydises were darn lucky her sister had bothered to make the effort, considering past history. This brother certainly needn't act as though it was the family doing Jill a favour, she thought aggressively.

She watched her sister's face, framed by its curtain of wispy ash-blonde hair which hung to her shoulders, and noted the tension written all over it with a further deepening of dislike for Andreas Karydis. She flicked back her hair, which was shorter than Jill's and cut to frame her face in a gleaming chin-length bob, as her soft full mouth tightened. Who did this family think they were, anyway? Royalty, by the look of it.

And then she cautioned the quick temper which her mother had always insisted came from her father's side of the family, and of which Jill had no trace. She didn't know what Andreas was thinking; she could have read all this wrong. Maybe the distant, aloof manner he had displayed with her and Jill was habitual with the man. Jill had told her that Theodore's argument with his family had begun long before he'd met her, but that when Theodore had chosen an English wife it had been the final straw.

That had been in the early days of her sister's marriage, and when she had asked Jill why Theodore had quarrelled so bitterly with his kith and kin and come to England, Jill had been vague and changed the subject.

It had been two or three years later before her sister had admitted Theodore had refused to discuss his past life with his wife, and that she had no idea what had caused the rift. Even Christos, whose name Theodore had been given by a friend of a friend back in Greece before he'd left his native land, and with whom Theodore had struck up an immediate rapport on seeking him out on arriving in England, did not know, according to Jill.

A mystery. And Sophy had never liked mysteries. Everything had to be clear and straightforward, as far as she was concerned; she couldn't have married Theodore for all the tea in China! Not that he would have asked her in the first place. A rueful smile touched her mouth. Jill's husband had always made it plain in a hundred little unspoken ways that he'd had as little time for her as she had had for him. She had just never been drawn to the strong, silent, macho type of male; Heathcliff might be great in the book but a dark, brooding, moody type of man would be sheer murder to live with, as far as she was concerned.

And then she came out of her reverie as, the luggage being in place on the trolley, Andreas turned and took Jill's arm, saying politely, 'Shall we?', his glance taking in Sophy and Michael before he strode off with Jill pattering along at his side.

Sophy smiled stiffly and hoped she hadn't betrayed the jolt her senses had given as the piercing eyes had met hers.

Strength and authority seemed to radiate from the man and it was too much, too overwhelming to be comfortable. Even the clothes he wore were a representation of the dark power that was in every glance, every gesture. All around them were colourful dresses and bright shirts, Bermuda shorts and cheeky tee-shirts vying with more elegantly flamboyant clothes worn by both sexes, but still undeniably cheerful and showy.

Andreas was wearing a brilliant white shirt, open at the neck, and plain charcoal trousers, and he was a monochrome of severity in all the brightness.

As they exited the building the full force of the June sun hit, the heat wrapping them round like a hot blanket, and Michael's awe-struck voice as he said, 'Wow! It's really, *really* hot,' brought his uncle turning round with a smile on his face.

'England is not so warm, eh?' he said indulgently, his tone of voice and the look on his face completely different with his small nephew than it was with the two women. 'It is normally in the eighties here in June, but even hotter in July and August. You will find yourself spending much time in your grandparents's swimming pool, I think. Like a little fish, eh?'

'A swimming pool?' Michael was elated, his big brown eyes shining. 'They have one of their own?' he asked in wonderment. He had recently learnt to swim at the local swimming baths and, although barely proficient, adored the water.

Andreas nodded. 'But one end is very deep,' he warned quietly, his eyes smiling into the little round face topped by a mass of curly light brown hair. 'You must never venture into the water unless you are with a grown-up, Michael. This is a rule for all the children who visit my parents's home, yes?'

'Who are the other children?' Michael asked immediately.

'Relations and friends of the family. Do not worry, little one. You will meet them all in good time,' his uncle said easily.

Andreas had been leading them across the vast car park as he had talked to Michael, and now, as he approached a long sleek limousine complete with driver, Michael's eyes nearly popped out of his head. 'Is this your car?' he asked breathlessly. Cars were his passion. 'Your very own?'

'Yes, do you like it?' Andreas asked, smiling at the enthusiasm.

Sophy had been viewing the light exchange between the two with something akin to amazement, and as she glanced at Jill she saw the same emotion in her twin's eyes. The youngest member of their little party was clearly not in the least intimidated by his formidable relation!

'It's beautiful,' Michael breathed reverently, stroking the silver metal with a respectful hand. 'And this is my favourite colour.' He walked round the car slowly, goggle-eyed.

'Mine too.' Andreas grinned at the small boy, and the two women exchanged a cryptic glance, reading each other's minds as they so often did. It looked as if Andreas and Michael were friends already.

The chauffeur had been busy piling the luggage into the cavernous boot of the vehicle, and now Andreas called him over, his voice composed as he said, 'This is Paul, my driver and also my friend.' As the small lean man smiled a smile which showed blackened teeth, Andreas continued, 'Mrs Karydis, Paul, and my nephew, Michael. And this is Miss...?' as he included Sophy in the sweep of his hand.

'Sophy Fearn. *Mrs* Sophy Fearn,' Sophy said, smiling sweetly into the gnomelike face of the driver. The 'Mrs' was a small victory, nothing at all really, but it felt wonderful to be able to trip Theodore's brother up on even a tiny detail.

There was a startled pause for just a second or two and then Andreas recovered immediately, his hard, handsome face hiding his thoughts as he said quietly, 'I do apologise, Sophy. I was not aware you were married but of course I should not have assumed.'

No, you shouldn't. Sophy held his eyes for just a moment, allowing her gaze to say the words she couldn't voice, and then she smiled coolly, her voice polite and unconcerned as she said, 'Not at all, Andreas, it's perfectly all right. And I'm a widow actually,' she threw in for good measure.

The grey eyes widened for a split second and again she knew she had surprised him. 'I'm sorry.'

Sophy was aware of Michael fidgeting at the side of them and knew her nephew was longing to ride in the car, and so she kept the explanation brief, merely shrugging as she said, 'My husband died three years ago and time helps.' She hoped, she did so hope he wasn't as crass as one or two of their friends had been with their sympathetic remarks after Theodore's death along the lines of, 'Such bad luck, the pair of you having such tragedies,' and 'I can't believe you've both lost your husbands,' as though she and Jill had been unforgivably careless.

But Andreas merely nodded, the compelling eyes holding hers for a moment longer before he opened the door of the limousine and helped them in, his manner formal in the extreme.

It was the first time he had touched Sophy, and the feel of his warm, firm flesh through the thin cotton sleeve of her light top was unnerving, although she wasn't quite sure why.

Once inside the overtly luxurious car, Michael's oohs and ahhs filled the air space and provided a bridge over any difficult moments, and then Paul was negotiating the big car out of the car park and they were on their way.

'Have you been to northern Greece before?' Andreas asked politely after a few minutes, his glance taking in both women.

'I haven't been anywhere,' Jill answered quickly, 'apart from a holiday in France with a load of other students when we were at university, but Sophy's always dashing off somewhere or other abroad with her job. She's used to travelling.'

'Really?' The dark gaze focused on Sophy's face.

'A slight exaggeration,' Sophy said quietly. 'I'm a fashion buyer so I have to pop over the channel now and again, and there's been the odd visit to Milan and New York, but most of the time I'm sitting at my desk with piles of paperwork in front of me.'

'A fashion buyer.' It could have been her imagination but Sophy thought she detected a note of something not quite nice in the deep voice. 'So you are a career woman, Sophy? An ambitious one?'

It was a perfectly reasonable question and if anyone else had asked it she wouldn't have minded in the least, but somehow, coming from Andreas Karydis, it caught her on the raw. 'I'm a woman in an extremely interesting job which I've worked very hard to attain and enjoy very much,' Sophy said coolly, 'but I don't care for labels.' It was dismissive but she kept it polite. Just.

She felt Jill shift uncomfortably at the side of her but Theodore's brother appeared quite unmoved, his eyes holding hers for a moment longer before he nodded unconcernedly, turning to Jill again as he said, 'I might be prejudiced, of course, but I consider this part of Greece one of the most beautiful. Halkidiki is mainly an agricultural area with pine woods and olive groves, and you'll find it's picturesque but with a timeless feel about it. In many places the people's way of life is still little affected by the twenty-first century, and the land is lush and green with wide open spaces and plenty of golden beaches. It is a pity you did not come in the spring; the fields are hidden under a blanket of flowers then, although they are still pretty in summer.'

'Have you lived here all your life?' Jill asked nervously after a few seconds had ticked by in silence.

Andreas nodded, and then the piercing gaze swept over Sophy's face for an instant as he said, his mouth twisting sardonically, 'But, like your sister, I travel a little. My father has olive, lemon and orange groves on his estate, but his main interest has always centred in shipping. Now he is older he prefers to take things easy and leave the main bulk of the Karydis business interests to me to handle. This suits us both.'

Jill nodded and said no more, but Sophy's mind was racing with a hundred and one questions she knew she couldn't ask. Was Theodore's family as wealthy as this car and the way Andreas had been speaking was making her think they were? Had Theodore been the younger or the elder son, and were there any more brothers and sisters? What had caused Theodore to leave this wonderful part of the world and make a new life in England? Question after question was presenting itself to her, but she forced herself to turn and look out of the car window as though she wasn't aware of the big dark man sitting opposite her, Michael at the side of him chattering away nineteen to the dozen.

They had been travelling along a wide dusty road with rows of cypress trees flexing spearlike in the faint hot breeze on either side, but now they approached a small village dozing gently in the noonday sun. The glare of whitewashed walls was broken only by purple and scarlet hibiscus and bougainvillaea, and chickens were pecking desultorily here and there at the side of the road, their scrawny legs only moving with any purpose when the limousine nosed its way past.

'Oh, there, Jill, look.' Sophy nudged her sister as she pointed to a spring some way from the road, where a collection of women had brought amphora-shaped earthen jars to collect the pure sparkling water, the overspill from the spring filling a trough from which a small brown donkey was drinking. 'Isn't that just lovely?' The two women were quite entranced.

'The water is quite untainted,' Andreas said quietly. 'Most of the villages have their own water supply plumbed in these days, but still the women prefer to come to the meeting place and chat and gather the water for their families in the time-old tradition. I think maybe very few people have the need to see the doctor for this epidemic called stress which is so prevalent in the cities, eh?' he added a touch cynically.

'Will I be able to drink from a stream like that?' Michael asked hopefully, 'at my grandparents's home?'

All attention drawn back inside the car, Sophy saw Andreas was smiling indulgently, his voice faintly rueful as he said, 'I'm afraid not, Michael. Your grandparents have all the conveniences of the twenty-first century, which includes water coming out of taps. However, if that were not so you would not be able to enjoy your own pool during your stay, so maybe it is not so bad?'

The village passed, the car took a winding road where the occasional stone house set among lemon, fig and olive groves broke the vastness of green fields baking under a clear blue sky.

'Why are those ladies wearing big boots?' Michael asked his uncle a few minutes later, pointing to where sturdy women were busy working in the fields, their legs encased in enormous neutral-coloured leather knee boots and big straw hats on their heads. 'Aren't they too hot?'

'It is for protection against the bite of snakes,' Andreas said soberly. 'It is not wise to work in the fields without them. This is Greece, little one. It is very different from England.'

He was very different too. Andreas was giving his attention to his small nephew, and it gave Sophy the chance to watch him surreptitiously. And she dared bet he was just as dangerous as any snake. How old would he be? She looked at the uncompromisingly hard handsome face, at the firm carved lips and chiselled cheekbones, the straight thin nose and black eyebrows. He could be any age from his late twenties right up to forty; it was that sort of face. A face that would hardly change with the years.

Theodore, at thirty-six years of age, had been eight years older than she and Jill, and in the last couple of years before his death had put on a considerable amount of weight and lost some of his hair. His brother was as different from him as chalk to cheese. But that happened in some families.

And then Sophy came to sharply as she realised he had finished talking to Michael and that he was looking straight at her, his eyes like polished stone and his eyebrows raised in mocking enquiry.

She flushed hotly, turning away and staring out of the window as her heart thumped fit to burst. He might *look* different, she qualified testily, but inside he was certainly a one hundred per cent Karydis, all right. Arrogant, cold, self-opinionated and dominating.

She had never understood what had drawn her sister to Theodore and how she could have remained married to him all these years, although once Michael had been on the way perhaps there had been little choice about the matter. Whatever, she couldn't have lasted a week, a day—an *hour* with him! And, although she was sure Jill was unaware of it, her sister was already beginning to lighten up a bit and show more evidence of the old Jill who had become buried under the authoritative weight of her husband.

This might be exactly what it was purported to be—a pleasant holiday for Jill and Michael to meet their in-laws and establish a long distance relationship for the future, but for herself she wasn't so sure about the purity of the Karydises's motives. And there was no way, *no way* she would stand by and see her sister come under the oppression of another dictator, be it Theodore's parents or his brother or the whole jam pack lot of them.

She straightened her shoulders and lifted her chin as though she was already doing battle. She would keep her eyes and ears open whilst she was here. She had always been far better than Jill at picking up any undercurrents, and she was doubly glad she had made the effort and accompanied Jill out here.

The Karydises might find Jill accommodating to a fault and somewhat naive, but they would discover her sister was a different kettle of fish if they tried to pull any fast ones!

CHAPTER TWO

IT WAS another half an hour before Andreas announced they were close to his parents's home, but the journey through the Greek countryside where the vivid blue backdrop of the sky had provided a perfect setting for small square white-washed houses with red tiled roofs, pretty villages and countless olive groves, and the odd dome-shaped spire dazzling in the sunshine, could have continued for much longer as far as Sophy was concerned. Apart from one factor, that was—the proximity of Andreas in the close confines of the car.

Since the moment he had caught her watching him she had been very careful to avoid any eye contact, but she knew without looking at him every time the grey gaze was levelled in her direction and it was unnerving. *He* was unnerving.

She hadn't met a man who exuded such a stark, virile masculinity before, and the open-necked shirt he was wearing had enabled her to catch a glimpse of the bronzed, hair-roughened flesh beneath which had caused her stomach muscles to tighten. And she liked that reaction even less than her earlier irritation and dislike because it suggested a kind of weakness.

It wasn't as though she *liked* the caveman type, she told herself crossly. Matthew had had the sort of looks she was drawn to: thick fair hair and blue eyes, a slim, almost boyish frame and classical fine features in an academic sort of face. Matthew had been gentle and mild, non-threatening, and that was her ideal man. Matthew. Poor, dear Matthew.

As the car turned off the main road into what was virtually a narrow lane, Sophy's thoughts were far away. She and Matthew had met at university and she had liked him right away. He had been funny and warm and easy to be with and, although at uni they had just been friends, once she had moved up to London—Matthew's home territory—their relationship had moved up a gear, and they had slowly begun to get to know each other better.

They had been married for just eight months before Matthew had fallen ill, and it had been a happy time. He had been her first lover and their sex life had been tender and comfortable, which had summed up their life together really, Sophy silently reflected, as the car came to a halt outside a pair of eight-foot-high wrought-iron gates set in a gleaming white wall.

And then, within two months of the liver cancer being diagnosed, Matthew had died, leaving her alone and utterly devastated.

Friends had rallied round and her job had helped, but it had been a full twelve months before she had felt she was beginning to enjoy life once again. And she hadn't dated since, in spite of several offers; shallow affairs weren't her style, and whether she had just been unlucky or men as a whole assumed a young widow was fair game she didn't know, but certainly the ones of her acquaintance seemed to assume a dinner and a bottle of wine meant a bed partner. And the married ones were the worst of the lot. It had been quite a disillusioning time, if she thought about it. She frowned to herself, oblivious of her surroundings.

'...Aunty Sophy?'

She came out of her reminiscences to the realisation that Michael's chatter had been directed at her for the last few moments and she hadn't heard a word. 'I'm sorry, darling,' she said quickly. 'I was day-dreaming. What did you say?'

But Michael was talking to his mother now, and it was left to Andreas to say quietly, 'He was merely pointing out the gates opened by themselves, courtesy of Paul's remote control of course.'

Sophy nodded, forcing herself to meet the level gaze without blinking. She noticed his grey eyes had turned almost silvery in the blinding white sunlight, throwing the darkness of his thick black lashes into startling prominence and yet earlier, at the airport, the grey had been nearly black. A human chameleon, she thought drily, and no doubt his nature was as enigmatic as his appearance. Some men liked to project an air of mystery.

More in an effort to show she was not intimidated than anything else, she said politely—the car having passed through the gates and into the spectacular gardens beyond—'It must be wonderful to live in such beautiful surroundings. Have your parents always lived here?'

'For the last thirty-two years,' Andreas said softly. 'I was actually born here twelve months after they first moved in.'

So he was only thirty-one; he seemed older somehow. And then her attention was taken by Jill who touched her arm, her voice awe-struck as she said, 'Look, Sophy, banana trees.'

They were travelling very slowly down a long winding gravel drive, the tyres scrunching on the tiny pebbles, and either side of the car was a cascade of vibrant colour. Masses of exotic, brilliantly coloured flowers and small shrubs were set strategically among silver spindrift olive trees, and the feathered leaves of jacarandas and the broad polished leaves of banana trees were also etched against the blue sky. The effect was riveting.

And then the car turned a corner and a long and very beautiful house was in front of them, its white walls and deep red roof perfectly complemented by the riot of colour at its many balconies, the same lacy ironwork reflected in the veranda which ran the full length of the house and which again had bougainvillaea, anemones, lobelia and a host of other trailing flowers winding over it.

'Oh, *wow*!' Michael, with the innocent ingenuousness of a child, verbalised what both women were thinking as he turned to his uncle, his brown eyes wide, and said, 'Are my grandparents *very* rich, Uncle Andreas?'

'Michael!' Jill turned as red as the scarlet roof. 'You mustn't ask things like that, darling,' she said reprovingly.

'Why?' Michael stared at his mother in surprise.

'Because it isn't polite.'

Polite or not, it was a pretty valid point, Sophy thought bemusedly. She could see tennis courts to the left of the house and Andreas had already mentioned the swimming pool; these people were *loaded*. She had always thought Theodore was nicely set up—what with his restaurant business and the lovely house he and Jill had lived in—but this, this was something else. Why hadn't Theodore ever said he came from such a wealthy family?

Jill must have had the same thought because her voice was small when she turned to Andreas and said, 'Theodore never talked about his family, Andreas, as I suppose you've guessed. You'll have to excuse our surprise.'

There was a moment's hesitation on Andreas's part, and then he surprised both women as he leant forward slightly, saying quickly under his breath, 'I understand this, Jill, but I would implore you not to reveal it to my mother. My father and I would expect nothing else, but she…she is desolate and it would serve no useful purpose to know he has not mentioned her to his wife and child. You understand?' he added urgently.

'Yes, yes of course.' Jill stared at Andreas as he settled back into his seat and then glanced once at Sophy.

Understand? She didn't understand anything about this family, Sophy thought militantly, but she was *so* glad she had come here with Jill. If the parents were anything like their offspring, they might soon be on the next plane home rather than enjoying a couple of weeks in the sun! Overwhelming wasn't the word for it.

However, she had no time to reflect further as the car had drawn to a halt at the bottom of the wide, semi-circular stone steps leading up to the house, and Andreas had already exited, turning to extend his hand as he helped both women out on to the immaculate drive.

The heat struck again with renewed vigour after the cool air-conditioning inside the limousine, but it wasn't that which caused the colour to flare in Sophy's cheeks. For a brief moment as she had slid out of the car and risen to stand beside her sister, she had been just a little too close to Andreas. Close enough to sense the muscled power in the big frame next to her and smell the faint, intoxicatingly delicious scent of his aftershave, and she couldn't believe how her body had reacted.

Fortunately the front door to the house was already opening and all attention was diverted to the couple standing framed in the aperture. 'There are your grandparents, Michael,' Andreas said very softly as he touched his small nephew on the shoulder. 'Would you like to take your mother and say hello?'

'Sophy?' Jill had turned to her, her hand reaching out, and Sophy said quickly, 'Take Michael and introduce him, Jill. I'm right here, don't worry.' She smiled encouragingly, her eyes warm, and after a split-second of hesitation Jill turned and did as Sophy had suggested leaving Sophy and Andreas standing together at the bottom of the steps.

That the women's swift exchange had not gone unnoticed by Andreas became clear in the next moment when, Jill and Michael now out of earshot, he said softly out of the corner of his mouth and without glancing down at her, 'So, it is true what I have read. I have always wondered if the text books are right.'

'I'm sorry?' Her voice was as quiet as his and Sophy
didn't take her eyes off her sister and nephew either. Immediately Jill and Michael had reached the couple standing
at the door to the house they had been enfolded in
Theodore's parents's arms; Michael's grandfather lifting
him up and hugging him to his chest, and Jill's mother-in-
law embracing the younger woman with an embrace which
looked to be welcoming. Sophy relaxed slightly.

'Dominant twin and submissive twin?' Andreas drawled
coolly.

It was less an observation and more an implied criticism,
and directed specifically at her. Sophy recognised it at once
and, true to her nature, rose instantly to the challenge. 'It
is both dangerous and naive to believe everything you read,
Mr Karydis,' she said icily, her eyes leaving the party
framed in the doorway and sweeping with cold dislike over
the dark profile next to her. 'I would have thought you
knew that?'

'So it is not true, then?' he returned evenly, the phantom
of a smile playing round the hard mouth suggesting he
found her attitude amusing rather than anything else.

She opened her mouth to fire back another put-down but
Jill was already turning back down the steps, calling her
name as she urged her sister to come and meet Theodore's
parents. All Sophy could do was to stitch a bright smile on
her face and keep it there during all the enthusing of how
very alike they were, and how *amazing* it must be to have
a mirror image, and so on and so on. But there was no edge
to Theodore's parents's greeting—unlike their younger
son's—and Sophy found herself relaxing still more. After
a little while the five adults and Michael entered the huge,
marble-floored hall behind them which was vast by any
standards.

Evangelos, Theodore's father, was an older version of
Andreas, but try as she might Sophy could see nothing of

Jill's husband in the tall, handsome man in front of her. And Dimitra, Theodore's mother, was not at all what she had expected. The doe-eyed and still quite exquisitely beautiful woman was clearly overjoyed to see her grandson and daughter-in-law and couldn't take her eyes off Michael. 'He is so like my Theodore at that age,' she said brokenly more than once, clutching hold of her husband's arm as though for support. 'You remember, Evangelos? You remember his curls and what a pretty child he was?'

Sophy saw Andreas and his father exchange a glance over the top of Dimitra's light-brown hair which was liberally streaked with strands of silver, and it was Andreas who gently walked his mother through to the beautiful drawing room off the hall, the others following with Evangelos.

'I am sorry.' Dimitra's glance included Sophy as well as Jill once they were all seated and she had composed herself. 'I just wasn't expecting Michael to be so like his father. It…it is wonderful, of course, but…'

As the older woman's voice trailed away and an awkward silence ensued, Sophy said quietly, 'Just at the moment a mixed blessing? But that will pass and it's perfectly understandable in the circumstances. Jill was only saying on the plane coming over that, having had Michael, she could understand a little of what you must be feeling.'

Jill flashed her sister a grateful glance and took her cue, moving off the sofa on which she and Sophy and Michael were seated and kneeling down in front of Dimitra before taking her mother-in-law's hands and saying softly, 'I would like us to be friends and for you all to get to know Michael, Dimitra. I know it won't take away the pain of your loss, but perhaps in time you could feel a little part of Theodore is still with you in the form of your grandson?'

'Oh, my dear…' Now the tears were pouring down

Dimitra's face as she held out her arms to Jill and Jill, still kneeling, hugged her mother-in-law.

Andreas cleared his throat before saying to a now silent and subdued Michael, 'How about if I show you the pool? You would like this? And also your grandfather has something in the garages that might take your fancy. Have you ever sat in a Lamborghini, Michael?'

'A Lamborghini? A real one?' Michael was over the moon.

'And there is a Mercedes too in your favourite colour,' Andreas told the small boy in a stage whisper, 'but don't tell your grandfather I've told you. Perhaps you and your aunt would like to come and see now and we can have a cold drink by the pool, yes?' The question was spoken in a tone which made it rhetorical.

Sophy stiffened slightly. It was one thing to remove Michael from the overwhelming emotions throbbing about the room, but from the way Jill turned and looked at her as Andreas spoke she knew her sister wasn't at all sure about being left alone with Theodore's parents, even if things did seem to be going well. And Jill was still the only person she was concerned about.

She squared her shoulders. 'I don't think—'

And then, to Sophy's surprise and anger, she found herself lifted up from the sofa by a determined, strong hand at her elbow. 'Come along, Sophy.' Andreas was smiling and his voice was soft and pleasant, but the granite-hard eyes were another matter. 'Ainka is going to serve refreshments in a few moments, so it is better I tell her now we will have ours by the pool in the sunshine. It is lovely there this time of the day.'

She glared her protest at his cavalier treatment. 'Now look—'

And then she found herself literally whisked across the room and out of the door, Michael padding along behind them, and it wasn't until Andreas had shut the drawing room door and had pointed down the wide expanse to his nephew saying, 'That door down there, Michael. That is the way,' that she came to her senses. And she found she was mad. Spitting mad.

'Let go of me, this instant!'

It was a soft hiss—Sophy was well aware of Michael's ever-flapping ears—but none the less vehement for its quietness, and Andreas immediately complied, his voice as low as hers as he said, as they both watched the small boy dance off down the hall, 'Your sister and my parents need time to themselves, Sophy. Surely you see that? This is an important time for them all.'

'What I *see* is me being man-handled and Jill left alone at a difficult time,' she snapped hotly. 'That's what I see! And who do you think you are, anyway, telling everyone what to do?'

'My parents's son,' he bit out with soft emphasis.

'And I'm Jill's sister,' she snarled with equal ferocity.

'What on earth do you think they are going to do to her in there?' Andreas asked testily, lifting a hand to Michael who had now reached the end of the hall and was waiting for them.

'I've no idea, have I?' Sophy returned cuttingly. 'Jill and I don't know you or your family from Adam! All we do know is that, for some reason, you all fell out with Theodore years ago and there's been no meeting point until now.'

'You cannot lay that at my parents's feet. My mother was inconsolable when he left Greece and would have done anything to bring about a reconciliation.' He glared at her, only moderating his expression when Michael called to them impatiently. 'And there was no "falling out" in the way you have suggested. My brother left Greece because

he wanted to and in the same way it was Theodore who
cut his family out of his life.'

'He had a family, Jill and Michael,' Sophy snapped back
quickly. 'And, from what I can gather, the fact that he
married my sister was the final nail in his coffin. Well, let
me tell you that he was lucky to get her! Darn lucky, in
my opinion. Jill is worth ten of any high society girl he
might have had paraded in front of him by your parents.'

'Now, look here—'

'I don't have to look anywhere, Mr Karydis. Jill might
be inclined to give you all the benefit of the doubt, but I
tell you here and now that my sister and Michael are my
only concern. I don't have to like you, any of you, and I
intend to make sure that Jill's good nature is not taken
advantage of. Now, you promised Michael a look at the
pool and the cars, so I think we should get on with it.' She
glowered at him, her eyes shooting blue flames, before she
turned to face Michael fully and arranged her features into
a more harmonious whole.

As she went to walk away, she felt his hand catch her
wrist again and she shot round to face him, grinding out
through clenched teeth, 'You touch me once more, just
once, and so help me I'll forget Michael is standing there
watching us and give you the sort of come-uppance you
should have had years ago.'

The stunned outrage on his face almost made her smile—
almost—but she was too angry to fully appreciate that it
was probably the first time Andreas Karydis had ever been
well and truly castigated. And by a mere slip of an English
girl at that.

As his hand dropped from her arm she swung round and
made her way to Michael—who was hopping about with
fretful eagerness—sensing Andreas was just behind her,
and then they were all entering a long corridor leading off
the hall. The kitchens were on one side and—according to

Andreas's terse voice—the resident housekeeper and the maid's private quarters on the other.

Andreas stopped to poke his head round the kitchen door and ask that their refreshments be served in the pool area, and then they continued to the end of the corridor and passed out of that door into the grounds of the estate and into hot bright sunshine.

Sophy let Andreas and Michael walk in front of her once they were outside for two reasons. One, she wanted to let Andreas establish a nice easy rapport with Michael for the little boy's sake and for the atmosphere to lighten generally, and two, she found she needed to dissect all that had been said and determine if she had been hasty at all. The truth of the matter was that she was feeling slightly guilty about some of what she'd said, and the more she went over their conversation in her mind the more she acknowledged she had gone too far.

She bit her lip as she glanced at the tall powerful man and small boy in front of her, the blistering afternoon sun beating down on one jet-black head and a smaller golden-brown one. Oh, darn it—what a way to set the ball rolling!

She had only been in Greece two minutes and she'd already dug a big deep hole for herself as far as Andreas Karydis was concerned! Not that it bothered her personally, if she was being truthful—he was a hateful, arrogant pig of a man and she thoroughly loathed him—but she was here as Jill's sister and Michael's aunt, and Andreas was Jill's brother-in-law and Michael's uncle. Unfortunately, the family connection was close.

They had almost reached the Olympic-sized swimming pool which glittered a clear blue invitation in the sultry heat but, although the magnificent surroundings and acres of landscaped grounds were breathtaking, their beauty was curtailed by her thoughts. Which had become clearer in the fresh air.

It was a less than auspicious start to their two weeks in Greece! Sophy groaned inwardly. But maybe Andreas wouldn't be around much anyway? They'd established earlier in the car that he had his own property some miles away, so apart from an odd call or two to be polite he probably wouldn't waste his time calling on his brother's widow and her sister.

But then there was Michael. And the two of them seemed to be getting on very well. Which was good—great, in fact. Of course it was. Or it would have been, if Michael's uncle had been anyone rather than Andreas! Oh, she didn't know what to think any more and she had a headache coming on. And it was all Andreas's fault.

'Why don't you sit down in the shade?' Andreas suggested as they reached the pool area and he turned round to look at her, his voice expressionless as he pointed to the far corner of the tiled surround where the dark shade produced by an overhanging and thickly blossomed tree was broken into patches by dappled sunlight. 'The sun can be fierce to the uninitiated.'

'Thank you.' It was stiff but the best she could do. The whole area was scattered with plump sun loungers and several tables and chairs, and she could see a vast brick-built barbecue in one corner and a pretty wooden sunhouse in another. Sophy glanced about her and then forced herself to say, 'This is very pleasant, idyllic in fact.'

He nodded, leading the way to a table and four chairs, and they had no sooner seated themselves than Christina, the plump little housekeeper, appeared, pushing a trolley containing an iced jug of lemonade and three glasses, along with a plate of sweet pastries and another of small rich cakes. A large bowl of fruit and several smaller bowls of different kinds of nuts and dried fruits was also placed before them, Christina smiling and nodding at them all before she ruffled Michael's curls and waddled back off to the house. It was some snack, Sophy commented silently.

'I like her.' Michael was blissfully unaware of the tense atmosphere as he helped himself to a nut-filled and honey-flavoured pastry. 'I like *everything* here.' He took a big bite of the sugared pastry before adding, 'Don't you, Aunty Sophy?'

Sophy sipped her lemonade and her voice was carefully neutral when she said, 'Yes, it's lovely, Michael.'

Andreas was looking at her, one eyebrow raised provocatively and she couldn't believe anyone could say so much without uttering a word. 'This is good,' he said gravely, 'as you have two whole weeks to enjoy everything.'

If there was one thing she loathed it was sarcasm, Sophy thought militantly, glaring again before she could stop herself.

As soon as Michael had finished his pastry he made his way to the pool edge, sitting down and removing his socks and shoes and dangling his feet in the water as he hummed a little tune to himself, completely happy for the moment as only children can be.

Sophy had had to restrain herself from stopping the child's move, but Michael's departure had somehow heightened the tense atmosphere to breaking point. She was almost relieved when Andreas said quietly, 'He seems remarkably well adjusted already to the loss of his father,' as he turned to look at her.

Sophy made the mistake of meeting the dark eyes trained on her face, and the way they all but pinned her to the spot brought a thudding in her chest which made her hand tremble slightly. 'They...they weren't close,' she said stiffly, wrenching her gaze away with some effort. 'Theodore spent most of his time working.'

In actual fact she had always felt Theodore was a severe father and that Michael feared rather than loved him, but she wasn't about to tell Andreas that. Besides, she could be wrong. She had only seen the two of them together a few times.

'You didn't like my brother.' It was a cool observation.

Surprised into looking at him again, she saw the intense eyes were narrowed and thoughtful but not hostile. Nevertheless she wasn't about to trust him an inch, and she stared at him for a moment before responding, 'What makes you say that?'

'Am I wrong?' he asked smoothly.

'He was Jill's husband and she loved him.'

'That's no answer,' he said softly.

'It is to me.' She raised her chin, her soft mouth tightening as he continued to study her with what Sophy considered to be intrusive intensity. 'The only answer you're getting.'

'You're very defensive about your sister's marriage,' he said at last, his body inclining slightly towards her as he spoke.

Was she? She didn't think she was, but certainly there was something about Andreas which made her uptight and on edge. 'No, I'm not,' she said sharply, moving her body irritably. 'But I happen to think their relationship was their own business.'

'I agree absolutely,' he said with silky composure, 'but if I remember rightly it was *your* attitude towards Theodore I was remarking on.' He smiled what Sophy considered a supercilious smile.

'And as you've only met me today and haven't seen your long-lost brother for years, I would suggest any remarks of that nature are extremely presumptuous,' she shot back quickly. Game, set and match.

He settled back in his seat, shifting his large frame more comfortably, and her senses registered the movement with acute sensitivity even as she steeled herself not to reveal a thing to the lethal grey eyes. He was very foreign, very alien somehow—far more than Theodore had been—but she didn't think it was altogether his Greek blood that made her feel that way. It was the intimidating nature of his masculinity, his bigness, the muscled strength which padded his shoulders and chest and the severe quality to his good looks. There was no softness anywhere, and in spite of herself she recognised such overwhelming maleness fascinated even as it threatened.

He looked cynical and hard and ruthless, but sexy too, very sexy. She bet he would be dynamite in bed.

The thought was such a shock that it literally brought her upright in her seat. She couldn't believe she'd thought it about him.

'What is it?' The grey gaze hadn't missed a thing.

'Nothing.' She forced her voice to sound cool and remote. 'But I would prefer to get back to the house now, if you don't mind.' She eyed him firmly, sensing what his answer would be.

'I do.' His voice was very smooth. 'There are still the cars to see, if you remember?'

'It's Michael who's interested in cars, not me,' Sophy said sharply, 'as you very well know. I don't want to see them.'

He stared at her with an enigmatic smile which didn't reach the cold intent eyes. 'That is a pity,' he drawled easily, 'because you are going to see them.'

'I see.' She was glaring again, she thought angrily, but she just couldn't match his irritating composure. 'Hospitality and putting a guest at ease aren't your strong points, are they, Mr Karydis?' Each word was coated in sheer ice.

He stiffened at her words and then laughed quietly, his face hard. 'Would you be offended if I said it depended on the guest?' he said with insulting politeness. 'Or that women like you make me think my countrymen were right to wait until 1952 before they gave the female sex the right to vote?'

'Oh, how very chauvinistic of you, Mr Karydis,' she said cuttingly. 'I gather you are one of those rather pathetic males who feel threatened by any woman who has a mind of her own and isn't afraid to use it? What's your view of the female sex? But no, let me guess. Our destiny is to be kept pregnant and barefoot, is that it? We're all supposed to fall into your strong male arms and beg you to make love to us?'

'If that is a subtle invitation, Sophy, you should wait to be asked,' he said reprovingly.

She knew it was a calculated jibe to get under her skin but in spite of that she couldn't disguise the furious anger his cool baiting had produced. It turned her cheeks scarlet and her eyes fiery as she spluttered, 'You, you—'

'Male chauvinist pig normally fits the description but you have already used that one,' he said calmly. 'However, being such a woman of the world I am sure you can find a more original definition if you try.'

He was laughing at her! It was there in the barely concealed curve of his lips and the glitter of amusement in the dark eyes, and Sophy would have given the world to be able to slap the smirk off his handsome face. But there was Michael just a few yards away, and it wouldn't do the little boy any good at all if his aunt suddenly attacked his new uncle, Sophy cautioned herself desperately. Although it would certainly relieve her stress levels.

And as though he had read her mind, Andreas added softly, 'Now, please, Sophy Fearn, do not force me to carry you kicking and screaming to the garages. It might upset the family.'

'And of course the family is everything,' she snapped hotly.

'Just so.' The grey eyes narrowed ominously. 'I care very

much for my parents and I am sure you care about your sister, so let us at least put on a facade of being civil, yes? It is only for two weeks, after all.'

Sophy drew on every little bit of will power she possessed and took a deep hidden breath. She had never met anyone she had disliked more—or so instantly. He was a brute, an arrogant brute, and she loathed and detested him, but this visit was not about her or her feelings. She had come to Greece to look after Jill and Michael and make things as easy as she could for them, and a feud with Theodore's brother simply wasn't an option in the circumstances.

She raised her chin a little higher, forced her voice into neutral and said flatly, 'I can manage two weeks if you can.'

'Excellent.' He rose to his feet and held out his hand to her. 'So, we will take Michael to see the cars and then return to the bosom of the family, yes? Smiling and calm.'

Sophy gritted her teeth as she ignored his hand and stood up. Thank goodness, thank *goodness* Andreas didn't live with his parents. With all the best intentions in the world, she didn't think she could have stood two weeks of seeing this man every day.

She looked at him as he walked across to Michael after a mocking smile, her senses noting the comfortable, almost animal-like prowl with which he moved. She felt shaky inside and that made her angry with herself. He had wound her up to screaming point and it was the first time she had allowed anyone to do that.

Unbidden, her mother's wedding photograph suddenly flashed onto the screen of her mind. She had found it one day when she was about eleven or twelve, hidden in the attic where she and Jill had been rummaging about when their mother had been at work. Their mother had spent nearly every waking hour working in an endeavour to keep a roof over their heads and food on the table, and although they had never wanted for anything on a material level the two girls had virtually brought themselves up.

From the time they had first asked questions about their father their mother had refused to discuss the man who had let her down so badly, but her bitter silence had spoken for itself. The twins had never dared to press the matter and they had assumed their mother had destroyed any photographs that might have been taken, so when they had discovered the picture of the handsome smiling man and his radiant happy bride they had pored over it for hours.

Their mother's fragile fairness had seemed even more delicate beside the tall dark man at her side, and she had been looking up at her handsome husband so adoringly, so reverently, it was clear to anyone how much she had loved him.

Their father had not been looking at his new wife but straight into the camera, his stance confident and self-assured and his handsome face wearing an expression of cool self-satisfaction which had bordered on the arrogant.

It had somehow fitted exactly the bare facts they knew— that their father had run off with a local beauty queen just a couple of months after they had been born, and had never bothered with them from that day on or even spoken to his wife again.

Jill had seemed to take the photograph in her stride but somehow, and Sophy couldn't have explained why, it had eaten into her soul like a canker. Their father had been aggressively handsome, very masculine and dark with a magnetism which had leapt off the paper. And she had hated him. Hated his swaggering bumptiousness, his insolent good looks and the dark charisma that had trapped her mother into a life of lonely, back-breaking hard work and embittered memories. He had ruined her life and he hadn't given a damn.

'Aunt Sophy? Come *on*.'

Michael's impatient, childish treble brought Sophy out of the dark void and into the bright June sunlight again, but for a moment she stared almost vacantly at the small boy standing in front of her. And then she forced herself out of the blackness.

'Uncle Andreas is going to take us to see the *Lamborghini*.' Michael clearly couldn't understand how anyone could fail to recognise the importance of this momentous event, and as Sophy looked down into the little eager face she found herself smiling and her voice was soft when she said, 'Lead on.'

As before, Sophy hung back and let the other two walk a few paces in front of her, and as she followed the large figure of Andreas and the small dancing boy at his side through an arched trellis wound with richly scented white roses, she found herself looking across a velvety smooth lawn which stretched beyond the pool area and curved back round the house in the distance.

The air was rich with the heavy, warm perfume of the scented bushes and landscaped flowerbeds surrounding the green area, and she noticed several flowered arbours complete with low wooden benches as they passed. It was like a stately home in England!

The Karydis family must have an army of gardeners to keep the grounds in such perfect condition, she thought idly as she walked on. Everything was immaculate.

Pristine tennis courts stretched behind the row of pretty red-roofed garages at the rear of the house, and Sophy stood looking into the distance as Michael oohed and ahhed behind her, climbing quickly into the Lamborghini and sitting agog as Andreas went through the controls with his small nephew.

Jill had unwittingly married into fabulous wealth, that much was for sure, but what on earth had made Theodore cut himself off from his family the way he had? Although Andreas seemed to have his brother's cold, authoritative nature, Evangelos Karydis had appeared quite warm and friendly and Dimitra even more so. Still, it was none of her business, not really, Sophy told herself silently. Only in as much as it affected Jill, that was. But one thing was for sure…

She turned and glanced back at the occupants of the Lamborghini, her face flushing in spite of herself as Andreas's eyes met hers for an instant, a disturbing gleam at the back of the grey. She was going to make very sure Jill made no commitment to this family, either in terms of herself or Michael.

She didn't trust these people, she didn't trust them at all, and the big dark man so deftly charming his small nephew at the moment she trusted least of all.

CHAPTER THREE

JILL was chatting quite happily when they re-entered the drawing room a little while later, and although Sophy was pleased to see her sister apparently relaxed and at her ease she felt a moment's disquiet too. Jill had always been the one to take everyone at face value and blithely assume people were as nice and straightforward as they appeared to be, and Sophy had picked up the pieces of her sister's trusting heart more than once when things had gone wrong when they were young girls. But this wasn't a case of schoolfriends being two-faced or a boyfriend letting her sister down. This was the Karydis family—Jill's in-laws and Michael's grandparents—and that was something very different. And it could be very dangerous.

Michael ran to his mother immediately, full of the swimming pool and the cars, and as Sophy stood in the doorway for a moment Andreas turned and looked straight at her. His voice was low as he murmured, 'Smile, Sophy. My parents will think you do not like them if you look at them like that, and that would never do,' but in spite of the silky sarcasm coating the words the threat underlying them was very plain.

She started slightly before she could control the action and then responded immediately to the challenge, her eyes fiery and her gaze fearless as she said, 'No one tells me what to do, Mr Karydis. Least of all you,' her voice as quiet as his but with a quality that made his mouth tighten. 'Remember that, will you?'

She had annoyed him. Good. Sophy brushed past him and walked across to the others, the satisfaction she felt at

43

puncturing his massive male ego just the slightest putting a smile on her face as she said politely, 'You have a beautiful home, and the grounds are quite magnificent,' as she glanced at Dimitra and Evangelos.

'Thank you, my dear.' Dimitra smiled back at her. 'And I understand you have been a tower of strength to Jill since—' She faltered and then swallowed quickly, continuing almost immediately, 'Since Theodore died.'

Sophy opened her mouth to make some polite social reply, but then as she looked into Theodore's mother's eyes she saw what Jill had seen. Pain, anguish, an almost tangible desperation that her son's wife and sister-in-law would like her, and it swept away anything but the desire to comfort the grieving woman in front of her. She sat down and then leant towards Dimitra.

'I've helped a little,' Sophy said gently, 'but I know how important it was to Jill to come here and meet you, and for Michael to get to know his grandparents.'

Dimitra's gaze moved to Michael as she murmured, 'So much lost time. So many wasted years and heartache.'

'But now Jill and Michael are here and this is a new beginning,' Andreas's voice said just behind Sophy, the warmth of his breath touching the slender column of her neck and making her shiver inside. 'Yes? And you will have many happy sunny days gossiping and putting the world to rights, no doubt.'

His voice had been tender, indulgent, and as different to the way he had spoken to her as it was possible to be, Sophy thought. But she didn't understand any of this. According to Theodore, the break from his family had become set in concrete when he had married an English girl, and yet here was his family welcoming Jill with open arms. Something didn't add up.

She continued to worry at the thought like a dog with a bone once the little maid, Ainka, had shown her to her truly

sumptuous room next to Michael's, Jill's being on the other
side of her son's. It had been suggested the two women
rested before they freshened up and changed for dinner at
eight. Andreas had offered to take Michael to the pool for
a swim—an invitation his nephew had accepted with alac-
rity—before the child had his own tea and was put to bed
by his mother, and now the house was quite silent.

Sophy lay down on the massive double bed the room
boasted but after five minutes or so gave up all thought of
a nap, and walked across to the wide glass doors leading
on to her balcony.

The luxurious bedroom and marbled en-suite were decorated in cool pinks and pastel blues and lilacs, reminiscent
of a bunch of sweet-peas, and the efficient air conditioning
had made the temperature comfortable, but as Sophy drew
back the gossamer-thin voile curtains and opened the doors
the heat struck with renewed force, reminding her she was
in a foreign country.

The balcony was furnished with a small table and two
chairs, and was a riot of colour with masses of white and
purple hibiscus and bougainvillaea winding over the
wrought iron, and tubs of scarlet geraniums set on the bis-
cuit-coloured tiled floor. The scent was heady and the tiles
were so hot they burnt her feet before she flopped down
on to one of the chairs with a little sigh of pleasure. This
was more like it!

She was wearing a thin, sleeveless summer dress which
she now hoisted up to her thighs as she stretched her long
legs out to the rays of the sun, letting her head relax back
over the edge of the chair as she shut her eyes and let the
warmth toast every bit of her. Gorgeous. Gorgeous, gorgeous, gorgeous. It would do Jill the world of good to relax
and soak up some sun for a couple of weeks, and it was
clear Michael intended to make the most of his unexpected
holiday. Perhaps things would work out?

And for herself? She continued to slump motionless in the chair as her thoughts moved on. She'd been in dire need of a break for months, if she was being honest. Although she and Matthew had decided a family wasn't for them for years, and that they would both put all their energies into their careers and then each other—in that order—it had been different after he had died. She had driven herself at a frantic pace then, and it had somehow become a habit. The rewards had been great, of course, and her job was certainly one in a million and she counted herself incredibly fortunate to be in such a position, but…nevertheless she was worn out. Exhausted. She hadn't realised just how much until this moment. She felt she could sleep for a week.

She must have fallen into a light doze because when she heard voices below the balcony it was as though she was emerging from thick layers of cotton wool. She opened her heavy lids slowly and moved just as cautiously as she silently straightened in the chair, wincing slightly as her neck muscles gave protest at the awkward position she'd adopted as she slept.

'Can we come to the pool again tomorrow, Uncle Andreas? Please? Can we?' Michael's voice, high with excitement, caused Sophy to peer through the screen of green leaves and flowers which hid her from sight as effectively as a small wall.

Michael was below, his curls wet and dripping and his small body gleaming like a baby eel's, but it wasn't her nephew who caused Sophy to become transfixed as her heart almost stopped beating and then raced in a most peculiar way.

Andreas was walking at the side of his small charge and he had clearly been more than a watchful bystander, as his brief—very brief—black trunks and the towel slung casually over one broad male shoulder indicated. His thickly muscled torso was tanned, and the black hair on his chest glistened with droplets of moisture before narrowing to a thin line bisecting his flat belly as it disappeared into the swimming trunks.

There wasn't a shred of fat anywhere on the hard, lean frame, nor on the powerful thighs or sinewy arms and legs. He was a magnificent male animal in the prime of life, and the easy way he was moving and the total lack of concern at the fact that he was as near naked as he could be showed how comfortable he was with his body.

Sophy was not comfortable. Anything but, in fact. She knew she was ogling him—there was really no other word for this shameful, clandestine spying—but once she had seen him she found she just couldn't draw her eyes away.

Growing up in an all-female household had caused her to be a little shy with the male sex in her youth, and Matthew's fair, almost hairless body had not prepared her for what she was seeing now. Nothing had prepared her for what she was seeing now! It was one thing to have the odd fantasy about idols of the silver screen, or indulge in a little imagining of how this icon or that would appear unclothed and in the flesh, but quite another to have that flesh—acres and acres of it, or so it seemed to her fevered gaze—hitting her between the eyes. Because that was what it felt like. And she couldn't ignore it.

She had been holding her breath in stunned fascination and then, as Andreas and Michael walked past on the ground below and disappeared into the house, she let it out in a long, low whoosh and sank back in the chair again, her heart pounding.

She held her hands up to her cheeks and discovered they were burning, which was ridiculous—*really* ridiculous— she told herself irritably. She wasn't some nervous little schoolgirl or a weak, trembling sort of female, for good- ness' sake.

Her career brought her into close contact with strong, determined and often ruthless individuals of both sexes, and she was used to dealing with any eventuality on a day to day basis. And she had been *married*; the male form held no mystery for her. At least she'd thought it didn't.

She bit her lip as she gazed over the balcony into the blue sky above, the sun now pleasant rather than hot as evening began to temper its heat. She wasn't going to think about this any more, she told herself firmly. She was going to go back into the bedroom and take a shower, and once she had washed her hair and sluiced away the strain of the journey—and Andreas Karydis—she would use lashings of the new, expensive body lotion she'd treated herself to just before leaving England.

She had well over an hour to pamper and titivate herself and she needed every minute because—and here her eyes became midnight blue—she intended to look like a million dollars tonight. She needed to show Theodore's brother that she was a cool, composed and sophisticated woman of the world and that all his nasty taunts and obvious dislike of her didn't mean a thing. She couldn't care less, in fact. He could be a cardboard cutout for all the effect he had on her!

She continued to tell herself the same sort of thing all the time she got ready for dinner, and by the time she popped in to Michael's room to say goodnight to the little boy the power of positive thinking had done its work. She felt like she could take on a hundred Andreases, especially when Jill's eyes widened and she breathed a 'Wow!' at the sight of her sister.

Michael was almost asleep and, after kissing him goodnight, both women tiptoed from the room. Once on the landing, Jill looked at her twin admiringly. 'You look absolutely sensational, Sophy. Is that one of the dresses from that collection in Paris you told me about?' she asked approvingly.

'Uh-huh.' Sophy grinned at her sister as she gave a little twirl, the coral gown of Fortuny-style pleats accentuated by Swarovski crystal hugging her slender figure. 'One of the perks of the job, although it still cost me an absolute fortune. I allow myself one extravagant purchase once in a blue moon, but this was the most expensive yet.' She rolled her eyes expressively.

Jill was still in her towelling robe, and now Sophy said, 'What are you going to wear tonight?'

'I'm not sure.' Unlike Sophy, Jill had never been the slightest bit interested in clothes, and it was fair to say that anything of any worth Jill possessed had been given her by her twin. 'Come and help me decide?' she entreated quickly.

Once in Jill's quarters, which were furnished exactly the same as her own but with a colour scheme of warm hyacinth blues and purples and sharp bright white, Sophy gazed at the clothes she herself had packed for her sister, Jill being unable to decide what to bring. Only something special would do.

'This.' Sophy extracted a pale lavender gown, the bodice of which was complemented by geometric paillette detailing in raw silk. 'We're going to knock 'em dead tonight, sis, or die in the attempt. Okay?' she said encouragingly.

'I haven't worn this since you gave me it,' Jill admitted with a feeble attempt at a smile. 'Oh, Sophy, I'm so nervous. Now I've had time to think, this is all out of our league, isn't it? I never dreamt Theodore came from such a background.'

'You got on fine with his parents,' Sophy reassured her firmly, 'and they seem to just be grateful you and Michael are here. Just be yourself, sis, and that will be enough, and take it from me—in these dresses we certainly won't look

like the poor relations. The Right Honourable Jill and
Sophy, more like!'

'Oh, Sophy.' But Jill was smiling now, and once she was
dressed sat chatting quite naturally while Sophy put her
sister's hair up in an elegant knot.

Ainka was waiting in the hall when the two women came
downstairs, and she led them to the huge ornate dining
room where the others were sitting just outside its patio
doors enjoying a cocktail in the dying sunlight.

'How charming you both look.' Dimitra's voice was gen-
uinely warm and her husband offered his own compliments,
but Sophy was too busy coping with what her first sight of
Andreas in evening dress had done to her senses. The scattered ones that remained, that was.

He's magnificent, she told herself silently. Magnificent
and threatening and dangerous. The formal clothes brought
a ruthless quality to the brilliant dark good looks that made
her shiver deep inside, and wish the evening was over
rather than just beginning. She'd been right, so right to be
wary of this man.

She heard him murmur something flattering to Jill before
Dimitra and Evangelos drew her sister to one side, asking
if Michael had settled down for sleep, which left her standing rather awkwardly at Andreas's side.

Ainka had handed her a large fluted glass of champagne
cocktail before leaving, and now Sophy concentrated on the
delicious effervescent drink as Andreas turned his pierc-
ingly dark and keen gaze on her, saying softly, 'You are a
credit to your profession and quite beautiful.'

'Thank you.' She smiled politely and took a sip from the
glass.

The words themselves were innocuous enough but there
was an edge to his manner Sophy didn't like, an edge of
criticism, although she wasn't going to give him the satisfaction of knowing she'd recognised it. She'd rather die.

'Do I take it you dressed Jill too?' he asked mildly.

'What?' She had turned her gaze away from him but now her eyes flashed to his dark face. She had been right. He was definitely put out about something.

'Your sister,' Andreas said smoothly. 'Clothed by Sophy Fearn? Or am I wrong?'

His accent was slight and his English was perfect, but the faint inflection it lent to the deep husky voice made her stomach muscles curl as she said tightly, 'No, you are not wrong, Mr Karydis. Do I take it you disapprove of what Jill is wearing?'

'Not what she's wearing, no,' he returned softly, 'just the motive behind it. *Your* motive, Sophy. And if you address me as Mr Karydis one more time I shall not be responsible for my actions. The name is Andreas, as you very well know.'

She ignored the latter comment, her chin well up and her voice icy as she said, 'So you credit yourself with mind-reading ability as well as everything else, is that it? Do explain, Mr Kar—' She stopped abruptly as the lethal grey gaze turned to shining ebony. 'Do explain,' she continued after a slight pause, 'my obviously base and wicked motives for giving Jill a super dress she could never afford otherwise—a dress, I might add, which was a birthday present six months ago,' she finished triumphantly.

'I'm not questioning your initial motivation,' he returned silkily. 'I'm sure you only wanted to bless your sister with a delightful gift and give her much pleasure.'

'Oh, thank you so much,' she cut in sarcastically. 'How kind.'

'But you encouraged her to wear the dress tonight because you look on my family as the enemy, an enemy which needs to be guarded against at all times. The dress was your way of pointing out that Jill has done very nicely

without us in her life—as is your attire, I might add.' He
eyed her imperturbably.

'What a load of nonsense,' Sophy lied vehemently, her
voice low enough for the others not to hear but carrying
forced outrage.

'Do you really think my parents wish to harm Jill or
Theodore's son?' Andreas asked quietly. 'Are you really
so poor a judge of human nature? They are generous,
warm-hearted people who have never knowingly hurt anyone.'

'Something which I'm sure can't be said of you,' Sophy
shot back before she had time to consider her words.

She stared at him, inwardly horrified but outwardly icy
calm as she waited for his reaction, and when it came it
wasn't the explosion she expected. 'So,' he drawled
thoughtfully, his hard mouth twisting slightly, 'it is me you
feel you have to armour Jill and yourself against. Yes?'

There was nothing she could say and so she merely
glared at him, her violet-blue eyes sparking. Hateful, *hateful* man!

'Have you always been such a fierce protector?' he
asked, his voice so soft now she could barely hear it. 'And,
if so, why did you let your sister marry my brother? He
could not have made her happy and certainly Michael has
no idea of what a father is.'

She was too amazed to hide her shock, but it was at that
moment Dimitra turned, calling them to join the others to
which Sophy responded with a promptness she knew was
not lost on Andreas. But she couldn't help it. Jill had been
right—they *were* out of their league here and she still
wasn't sure what was going on. This family was like a
proverbial minefield.

Sophy had downed two champagne cocktails before
Ainka called them into dinner, but she felt she needed a
little Dutch courage. She knew every time Andreas's dark

eyes flashed over her and it was often, often enough for her to feel constantly shaky inside. That in turn made her angry with herself and churned her stomach still more. Which was ridiculous, darn it. He was just Theodore's brother.

Jill, on the other hand, was chatting away to Dimitra as though the two of them had known each other all their lives; Evangelos looking on indulgently and joining in the women's conversation now and again. In fact, everyone seemed at ease and relaxed apart from her, Sophy thought irritably.

But it would be better once Andreas left. She supposed she should have expected Theodore's brother would be around for the first few hours, but having his own home meant he would just call by now and again. Didn't it? She prayed it did, Sophy reiterated as she finished the first course—a delicious soup made with yoghurt and garlic and fresh vegetables—and looked at the dishes Ainka was piling on to the table.

She was sitting next to Dimitra with Jill opposite her and Andreas at the side of Evangelos, who was heading the table, so she had found it easy to avoid the granite-grey eyes. Nevertheless Andreas's dark, brooding presence had the effect of making her all fingers and thumbs, and when she knocked over her wine glass—white wine, fortunately, and not red—she wasn't really surprised. The whole evening was an accident waiting to happen!

'Oh, your beautiful dress.' Dimitra looked aghast at the puddle in Sophy's lap, which Sophy was hastily mopping with her table napkin. 'You must sponge it down with water or it will stain.'

'It's all right, really.' She knew her face was fiery but she was so furious with herself she could scream. So much for the calm, cool, cosmopolitan woman of the world, she thought bitterly as she felt the wine soak through to her panties. Talk about pride going before a fall! What on earth was Andreas thinking?

What he was thinking became evident in the next moment when he rose to his feet, pushing back his chair with the backs of his legs before walking round the table and drawing her up with an authoritative hand at her elbow.

'Come and repair the damage in the downstairs cloakroom,' he said in a tone which left her no choice but to obey when married to his grip on her arm. 'It won't take a moment and it would be a shame to spoil such a delightful dress.'

Was she the only one who could hear the sarcasm in his voice? Sophy asked herself as she submitted to being led from the room with as much grace as she could muster. Apparently so, from the smiles and nods from the others. They clearly thought Andreas was playing the perfect gentleman. The manipulative swine!

She waited until they were in the hall and the dining room door was closed before shaking off his hand with enough venom to make the dark eyebrows rise. 'Thank you, I can manage perfectly well now,' she said stiffly. 'I've dealt with worse than this before.'

'Oh, I have no doubt you can look after yourself, Sophy,' he said from his vantage point of six foot plus, staring down at her delicate fairness with hooded eyes. 'You might look as though a breath of wind would blow you away, but there is a backbone of steel in that fragile frame, is there not?'

'Don't tell me, you disapprove of that too!' she returned frostily. No doubt he was one of those men who preferred his women to be for ever batting their eyelashes and playing dumb. She knew his type all right.

'Did I say that?' he asked in a tone which suggested suppressed amusement. 'Now, be fair, did I?'

Nothing could have got under her skin more than to think he was laughing at her, and her voice sharpened as she said,

'You didn't have to. You can say talk more effectively without saying a word than anyone I've ever met.'

'Another snap decision.' He stood back a pace, folding his muscled arms and staring down at her for a second or two as she glared back at him. 'What a little harridan you're going to be in a few years,' he observed nonchalantly, before taking her arm again and whisking her over to a door to the right of the dining room which he opened with his free hand. 'The cloakroom,' he stated unnecessarily as Sophy surveyed a room large enough to swallow at least half of her little London flat. 'Now, let's see about getting you cleaned up.'

In spite of his comment about the backbone of steel he was making her sound as though she hadn't got a grain of sense, Sophy thought furiously, her anger blinding her to the fact that Andreas had entered the cloakroom with her until it was too late to protest. She stared at him as he casually began to fill one of the bowls—of which there were three—with cold water. 'What are you doing?' she managed at last.

'Cold water is best for white wine.' He raised innocent eyebrows.

'I'm not referring to the wine stain,' she said tightly. As he very well knew. 'I'm perfectly capable of sponging down my own dress.'

'What kind of host would I be to let you struggle alone?' he countered with a charming smile which didn't fool Sophy in the slightest, especially when she looked into those glittering eyes.

'I'd prefer to struggle, actually.'

'Sophy, you are a guest in my parents' home.'

The eyebrows were raised again, she noted irritably, and they made her feel like an errant child who was having a tantrum. 'So?' she snarled tightly. What had that to do with anything?

'So I am not about to…abuse that position,' he murmured gently, the soothing tone positively insulting.

'I didn't think for a moment you were!' It had the added advantage of being absolutely truthful, something Andreas couldn't fail to recognise. 'Of course I didn't.'

He stared at her for a long moment and by the end of it Sophy had to grit her teeth in order not to look away. He had been leaning against the wall whilst they talked, and now he levered himself upright, his eyes taking on a distinctly pewter quality as he ground out, 'You really are the most—' before stopping abruptly, and visibly controlling himself.

'The most what?' she countered swiftly, her defiance strengthened by the fact that she couldn't see he had anything to complain about. She had agreed with him, for goodness' sake! That was a first if nothing else. And she hadn't accused him of trying to take advantage of her—just the opposite, in fact. What was the matter with the man? He disliked her as much as she disliked him, she knew that, so why was he all bristling male ego?

'Forget it.' It was cold and abrupt. 'Just forget it.'

'No, hang on a minute.' As he turned to go, she caught at his sleeve, a tiny part of her amazed at her temerity. 'You obviously have something to say, so say it.'

'It doesn't matter,' he bit out grimly. 'You are Jill's sister and I am Theodore's brother. That is all. We are bound through family ties to get on with each other as well as we can over the next little while. If you would like to deal with the matter of the dress, I will then escort you back to the dining room,' he added with stiff formality. 'I will wait outside.'

She could feel bunched muscles under her fingers and, unbidden, a picture of how he had looked earlier, tanned and dark and uncompromisingly virile, made her breathless and took any tart rejoinder she might have made straight out of her consciousness.

She remained staring at the door to the cloakroom a good ten seconds after Andreas had left, and then roused herself to get to work on the dress. The material was wafer-thin, as was the lining, and after sluicing handfuls of cold water over the stained area she patted it carefully with one of the cloakroom's fluffy towels which dried it almost immediately.

The recovery mission accomplished, Sophy stared at her reflection in the full-length mirror for a few moments. She was too flushed, she decided critically. Too bright-eyed. It was the champagne, of course, that was *definitely* all it was, but she had better dab her hot cheeks with cold water before she went back to the others.

By the time she opened the cloakroom door she was feeling a little more like herself, and when Andreas levered himself off the opposite wall where he had been waiting for her she managed a fairly cool smile as she said, 'I'm sorry to have kept you waiting but there was no need for you to stay.'

'It is no problem.' His gaze was remote, implacable, and it made her want to gabble. Instead she kept her mouth tightly shut as they walked back to the dining room, and it was only when she sat down in her chair and felt taut muscles relax that she realised just how tense she had been.

The meal was wonderful, and as course followed course Sophy realised Christina's cooking was first class. The housekeeper made an appearance at the end of the dessert stage when she bustled into the dining room with the coffee, Ainka following with a tray containing a carafe of ouzo—a spirit distilled from grapes—and another of iced water.

Sophy had been hoping she could escape to her room; the slow leisurely style of the last meal of the day in Greece meant they had been at table for over two hours. And two hours of Andreas Karydis was enough for anyone!

But as Christina poured a cup of the heavy sweet coffee for everyone and Ainka filled the women's glasses with iced water and those of Evangelos and Andreas with ouzo—the women having declined the spirit—she realised she had at least another half an hour or so of social chit chat to get through, just to be polite. And, the thing was, she wouldn't have minded if it was just Theodore's parents and herself and Jill present, but Andreas's dark presence on the perimeter of her vision was keeping her as jumpy as a cat on a hot tin roof. And he knew it too.

At half-past ten, when her nerves were stretched to breaking point, she rose jerkily to her feet. 'I hope you'll excuse me, but I have a slight headache,' she said politely to the room in general, allowing her glance to brush each face briefly before it concentrated on that of Dimitra's. 'I think I'll turn in, if that's all right. Thank you for a lovely dinner and for making me so welcome,' she added with a warmth which was quite sincere. 'It was really very kind of you to include a third party in Jill's invitation, and I do appreciate it.'

Through the ensuing effusive reassurances from Evangelos and Dimitra that *of course* she was very welcome in their home, and that as Jill's dear sister she *must* count herself just as much a part of their family as Jill and Michael, Sophy was very aware of the cool scrutiny of the tall dark man standing watching her across the other side of the table, although she ignored him.

Andreas had risen when she had stood up—he had the social etiquette down to a fine art, if nothing else, Sophy reflected a trifle nastily—but he hadn't added his voice to those of his parents. Not that she had expected him to do so.

He simply stood there, silent and enigmatic, his glittering

gaze trained on her flushed face and his big body relaxed and still, looking at her as though he was a scientist studying some rather repellant bacteria under a microscope.

Sophy smiled again, wished them all goodnight in as bright and carefree a voice as she could manage and left the room quickly, forcing herself to restrain the urge to break into a trot once she was in the hall and making her way towards the stairs.

'Awful man. Awful, awful, *awful* man.' She found she was muttering to herself once she had reached the sanctuary of her room and stopped abruptly, kicking off her high heels as she walked over to the bed and flung herself down on the soft covers with a little sigh of exasperation.

She couldn't let Andreas get to her like this. She had only been in Greece for a matter of hours and here she was all knotted up and at loggerhead with Jill's brother-in-law. And she was supposed to be here to *help* Jill and Michael, to smooth their path as it were—not enter into war with a member of the family.

They had got off on the wrong foot, but hopefully, now he had made the polite overtures of welcome his parents had obviously required of him, his presence at the house would be minimal. And if Dimitra and Evangelos were really as pleasant as they appeared to be, the next two weeks might roll by quite happily.

But it was strange… Sophy's clear, unlined brow wrinkled as she rolled over on to her back and gazed up at the pale blue ceiling which had rather impressive little fat cherubim fashioned in each of its corners. As far as she could recall, apart from those first few minutes when they had arrived at the house, Dimitra and Evangelos had mentioned their eldest son hardly at all. Now that wasn't normal in the circumstances, was it?

She had left the balcony windows open whilst she went down to dinner and now, as the thin, flimsy drapes moved with the warm evening breeze, she heard the sound of voices from somewhere outside. Andreas must be leaving, but as the drive was at the front of the house and her room was situated at the back overlooking the landscaped grounds, beyond which stretched the swimming pool, she could distinguish little of the conversation beyond Evangelos's voice calling something in Greek, probably goodbye.

It was quite dark outside, but once on the balcony Sophy breathed in the rich scented air and looked up at the moon brushed free of clouds. She felt restless tonight, and although she hadn't lied about the headache she didn't feel like going to sleep. She massaged her aching temples slowly.

The night was soft and warm, a night for lovers, for passion. A night for endless caresses and whispered promises, for reaching the heights.

And then she caught hold of her errant thoughts sharply, utterly amazed with herself. What had got into her tonight? she asked herself bewilderedly. She must have had too much wine. Why was she feeling so disturbed and edgy, fretful even? This wasn't like her. She was always perfectly in control of herself.

She heard the sound of a car's engine and the scrunching of tyres on the drive which signalled Andreas's departure, either by taxi or maybe he had called out his driver to pick him up. Whatever, he was leaving and that was the main thing.

But with Andreas's name came the clear picture of how he had looked that afternoon after leaving the pool—tanned, dark, virile, dangerous.

And suddenly Sophy knew why she was feeling the way she did.

CHAPTER FOUR

AS WITH every other unpleasant thing which had come her way in her twenty-eight years of life, Sophy faced the fact that she was sexually attracted to a man she thoroughly disliked head-on.

It was galling in the circumstances, and she could just imagine the satisfaction Andreas would feel if he knew—which meant he must never find out. What made the situation all the more unpalatable was that she had never felt this way before and she couldn't understand why it had happened now, so fiercely and without warning. And with Theodore's brother, of all people.

She paced the bedroom, her eyes stormy and her mouth tight with self-deprecation. The truth of the matter was she had never met a man with such lethal magnetism before, she admitted after a good ten minutes of self-analysis, not in a day-to-day setting of close contact anyway. Oh, there had been the odd male on the Tube or at a function or something, whose good looks had had that extra dimension which had made her heart beat faster, but not like this. Not like Andreas Karydis.

But it didn't matter. It didn't, not really. She was panicking because she felt things were out of control—but they weren't, *they weren't*, she reassured herself grimly. Everything was fine. All her life, from when she had been a little girl of three or four and had realised she and Jill hadn't got a daddy like everyone else—and moreover that there was something shameful and secret about the fact, judging from her mother's reaction when they asked questions, she had imposed an almost obsessional self-control on herself.

And when she had found out the truth about her father
and had seen what loving and trusting a man to distraction
could do to a woman, she had consciously vowed she
would never let herself be manoeuvred into such a humiliating position. Life—her life—was built on constraint and
determination and absolute autonomy, and within those re-
straints she was happy. She had met and married Matthew,
hadn't she? And they had been united in agreeing each of
them would follow their own separate career and destiny
within their relationship. It had worked. It would still be
working if he hadn't died.

She stopped her pacing and walked into the bathroom,
turning on the shower before slipping out of her clothes
and allowing the cool silky water to bathe her hot skin.

She was just overtired, that was all. Theodore's death,
the awful funeral and trying to support Jill and Michael at
the same time as giving her job the hours it needed had
taken it out of her. She worried about Jill, she couldn't help
it.

She had always felt more like Jill's mother than her sister, she reflected ruefully as she lifted her face to the re-
freshing spray. And although she had always tried to hide
her concern about Jill's choice of husband, her initial misgivings had grown with the years rather than decreased.

What had Andreas meant with that crack about
Theodore? She frowned as she tried to remember his exact
words. Oh, yes, he had said Theodore couldn't have made
Jill happy and that Michael had no idea of what a father
was. She would ask him what he meant by that, the next
time she saw him. He couldn't make remarks like that without explaining himself fully, and there was a sight too much
cloak-and-dagger stuff concerning Theodore, in her opinion!

Once back in the bedroom and with sleep a million miles
away, Sophy picked up one of the novels she had brought

with her from England, climbed into bed and adjusted herself comfortably against the heaped pillows. She would read for a few minutes before settling down to sleep, she decided, and put all thoughts of a certain tall, dark Greek out of her mind.

An hour later she was more wide awake than ever and couldn't remember a line she had read. The book could have been written in double Dutch for all the sense it had made to her whirling mind. She threw it down irritably, annoyed with herself.

She had heard Jill come upstairs just after Andreas had left, and some time after that all the lights had been extinguished downstairs and now there was only shadowed blackness beneath the balcony windows. The whole house was asleep. The whole *world* was asleep, she told herself restlessly, wondering why it was always so much worse to be awake when you knew everyone else was sleeping peacefully.

She settled herself down, resolutely switching off the lamp at the side of the bed. She *was* tired and her body was calling out for rest; it was only her mind that seemed determined to solve all the problems of the universe!

After half an hour of tossing and turning, the light went on again and Sophy swung her legs out of bed, her face frowning. Okay, so she couldn't sleep, but she'd go stark staring mad if she had to remain in this room another minute. She would go for a walk in the gardens. In fact, she could take her swimming costume with her and if there was enough light she could perhaps have a swim in the pool. It was as warm as a summer's day in England.

The decision made, she dressed quickly in light cotton combat trousers and a thin but warm cashmere jumper she'd brought with her, just in case the night was a little chilly after the intense heat of the day. After grabbing a towel and her costume, and slipping on a pair of flat pumps, she opened the door to her room cautiously and peered out on to the landing. Everywhere was silent and dark. She felt a moment's trepidation which she ignored.

She made her way carefully downstairs by the light of the moon shining through the windows, and then paused in the massive hall, suddenly uncertain. What if the place was alarmed and she roused the whole house?

Well, she'd just explain she was hot and bothered and had decided to take a midnight swim, she told herself firmly. And with the huge wall surrounding the property and the fact that Evangelos's estate was miles from the nearest village, there probably wasn't an alarm anyway.

There wasn't. In fact, the door at the end of the corridor leading off the hall wasn't even locked, and Sophy passed quietly through into the cool scented darkness of the night with no trouble at all, breathing a little easier now that hurdle was over.

Once outside, she found the moonlight was lighting up the grounds almost as bright as day and her way was quite clear. She breathed in the perfume of the sleeping vegetation in great gulps as she walked down towards the pool, suddenly finding herself grinning. This was great, quite an adventure, and it had been years since she had acted on impulse.

Her footsteps quickened as she lightly skimmed the lawn and ran down through the arch of roses into the pool area, and after kicking off her pumps she had stripped off the trousers and jumper and donned the swimming costume in seconds. The pool appeared even more enormous in the moonlight, and the far end under the trees was in deep shadow which caused her a moment's disquiet before she told herself not to be so silly. She walked to the shallow end of the pool as the cool breeze drifted over her skin and ruffled the silk of her hair.

She dipped her toe in the water and then squeaked as the cold water hit her nerve-endings. It felt *freezing*!

She was just about to jump in, knowing it would take ages if she tried to do it gradually, when something—a movement, a ripple or maybe just her sixth sense—caused her to pause, her heart beginning to thump madly as she peered into the blackness.

'Is…is anyone there?' She felt slightly ridiculous speaking to thin air, but something wasn't right.

Nothing happened for what seemed like an hour but in reality was no more than a second or two, and then an unmistakable voice said quietly, 'It's me, Sophy. Andreas.'

Andreas? *Andreas?* She heard the swish water made when a body was cutting through it and then after a moment saw a dark shape come out of the shadows and into the tiny glittering waves lit by moonlight. And in the same instant she glanced over at the chair where she'd thrown her clothes and awful realisation hit. She'd thought she was alone and she had been completely naked for a few moments. Had he seen? What was she thinking? *Of course* he had seen. A blind man would have seen!

'You rotten, low, conniving—'

'Hey, hey.' He paused to tread water in the middle of the pool, his face shadowed planes and angles in which only the glitter of his eyes was truly discernible. 'What have I done now?' he asked with every appearance of hurt surprise.

'*What—?*' Words failed her and she had to take a hard pull of air before she could continue. 'What have you done? You know *exactly* what you have done, so don't come the old soldier with me,' she bit out furiously. 'You let me change into my costume without a word to warn me you were here. You're absolutely disgusting!' she finished scathingly.

'I didn't even see you until it was too late,' he said

mildly. 'You flitted in here like a breath of moonlight and proceeded to whisk off your clothes in two seconds flat. When I realised I was no longer alone, you were already…'

'Naked!' she spat angrily.

'In a word, yes.' He swam closer, hard muscled arms slicing through the dark depths to emerge briefly in the moonlight, silver and gleaming. 'Is it my fault you are one uninhibited lady?' he drawled softly when he was closer.

'I am *not* uninhibited,' Sophy hissed furiously, bitterly resenting the innuendo that she was quite happy to take off all her clothes in front of a virtual stranger.

'So you're inhibited?' he asked in tones of hateful sympathy.

'No, of course I'm not.' She glared at him and then stamped her foot. 'And don't try any of your mind games on me, Andreas Karydis,' she warned furiously. 'I know your little tricks.'

'That's an improvement.'

'What?' She glared at him, resenting the easy tone.

'You actually called me by my first name. Of course, the Karydis came after, but I still count that a step forwards.'

She just didn't believe this man. She stared at him before drawing herself up and saying icily, 'You can count it any way you want, but I still think you're disgusting. To spy on people like that! It's totally beyond the pale.'

'I wasn't spying on you, Sophy,' he said silkily. 'Any more than you were on me earlier.'

'Me?' He couldn't, he *couldn't* know about that?

'On your balcony?' he reminded her gently. 'You happened to be there and I happened to be underneath; I understand that perfectly. And tonight I happened to be in the pool and you…' He let his voice die away and smiled up at her instead.

Sophy had always considered herself a very non-violent person but right at this moment she wanted to commit murder. 'That is utterly different and you know it,' she managed through gritted teeth. 'There was no time for me to make myself known.'

'My point exactly,' he said appeasingly.

His hair was wet and black and he raked it back with one hand as he stood up, the water now reaching to just above his waist. His eyes hadn't left hers but he made no attempt to get out of the water, perhaps sensing she would run if he did.

'I...I'm going back to the house,' she said tightly. 'I didn't come down here to bandy words with you.'

'Of course you didn't,' he agreed smoothly. 'You came here to swim, so swim. No one is stopping you.'

Oh, yes, they were. The swimming costume she had brought with her was a modest one-piece affair in black lined silk. It was perfectly decent but she almost felt as naked as she had been a few minutes earlier with those lethal grey eyes fixed on her.

His maleness was even more flagrant in the dark shadows of the pool and, far from being chilly as she had been a few minutes before, she now felt feverishly hot. She wanted to moisten her dry lips but, knowing he would read the gesture for what it was—nerves—she restrained the impulse, and said instead, 'I came here to be alone, actually.'

'Don't be childish.' He turned in the water as he spoke, taking off for the deep end with a ruthlessly powerful drive. 'There's plenty of room for both of us in here, and I promise I won't talk to you or interfere with your swim in any way. Okay? Does that satisfy you?'

No, it didn't satisfy her at all, but Sophy felt as though she were between the devil and the deep blue sea, or perhaps the devil and the deep blue swimming pool was more correct.

She was still in the same position when Andreas swam back, his voice decidedly mocking now as he said, 'Frightened of the big bad wolf, Sophy? Is that it? Believe it or not, I have actually seen a woman naked before and the sight of your body—although undeniably a nice bonus on a night like this—will not turn me into a sex-crazed monster. You'll be quite safe.'

Impossible man! But the overt derision settled the matter and when he again turned and swam away Sophy wasted no time in entering the water. Once the first shock of the cold had abated she found it was pleasant, and after three or four lengths of the pool when she steadfastly ignored the dark figure cutting backwards and forwards in the opposite direction to her she found she was quite warm.

However, after some ten minutes or so in the pool, when Andreas had said not a word, the silence had become so loud Sophy felt like screaming to break it. Instead, at the point where their bodies passed each other, she said a trifle breathlessly, 'I thought you had gone home. There was a car earlier?'

'That was my driver, Paul, arriving, not me leaving.'

'He's here too?' For a moment she almost expected the little gnome like man to pop out from behind a bush.

'There were some papers I wanted my father to look at tonight before he went to bed, and it was easier for Paul to bring them and a change of clothes for me so we could go straight to the office from here in the morning,' Andreas explained briefly, before swimming in the opposite direction.

His eyes had been black in the shadows and the bulk and breadth of him somewhat alarming so close to, his teeth gleaming white and the drops of liquid on his face and hair catching the moonlight as he had talked. Sophy felt a stirring in the pit of her stomach, a flood of sexual awareness that was impossible to deny. She continued on her route, splashing a little more than was necessary as her arms and legs seemed unable to follow the commands of her brain.

Andreas spoke the next time they passed. 'You couldn't sleep?'

'No. There's been so much happening today and, I suppose, a strange bed and all that...' Her voice tailed off breathlessly.

'I never have a problem sleeping in a strange bed,' Andreas said huskily, the gentle teasing in his deep voice causing her further problems with her coordination.

She just bet he didn't, Sophy thought hotly as they went their separate ways again. A woman in every port, if she knew anything about it. *Several* women in every port, in fact.

'Don't overdo it on your first session.'

'What?' This time she did actually swallow a mouthful of water and spluttered a bit before she could say, 'I was just thinking about getting out, actually.' Away from his disturbing presence.

'So was I,' Andreas said immediately.

'Oh, right.' Brilliant. She had been hoping to exit fairly gracefully and hurry back to the house whilst he was still in the pool. She had noticed this swimming costume, which was quite proper and respectable when dry, seemed to have taken on the effect of a second skin when wet, clinging to every curve and contour with a determination that was positively wanton. And she knew exactly what would happen when her breasts met the cool night air; her nipples were already hardening and stretching the silk still more.

She scrambled out of the pool with more haste than aplomb, conscious of Andreas in the water behind her, but once she had grabbed her towel and wrapped it round her sarong-fashion, she found the nerve to turn and face him. She was surprised to see he was still in the pool with something of a winsome expression on his hard handsome face. 'What's the matter?' she asked cautiously. Why wasn't he getting out?

'A slight problem.' He sounded quite cheerful as though it wasn't really a problem at all. 'I thought I would be alone down here, you see.' He smiled innocently.

'So?' She stared at him, puzzled. What was he saying?

'So...no trunks,' he said with magnificent matter of factness.

'No *trunks*?' She had been swimming with a naked man—and not just any old man, either, but Andreas Karydis! 'What do you mean, no trunks?' And then, as he went to get out of the pool she added hastily, 'No, stay where you are. I know what you mean. I just don't know why! Why you didn't tell me at first, that is.'

'Because you would not have come into the pool and you have enjoyed your swim, yes?' he answered silkily. 'Have you not ever...how do you English say, skinny-dipped?'

'No, I have not,' she answered a trifle indignantly. What did he take her for, anyway? 'It's not exactly encouraged in the local baths in London,' she added caustically.

'But when you have been abroad?' he persisted softly. 'Not then?'

'On a beach with hundreds of other people? I think not,' she said hotly.

'Ah, yes, I see your point,' he agreed thoughtfully. 'Then you must indulge whilst you are here, Sophy. It will be quite safe late at night down here. No one comes.'

'You came tonight,' she reminded him tightly.

'Ah, yes.'

'Where's your towel?' she asked feverishly, glancing round as though it was going to come hopping towards her of its own accord. What a ridiculous situation to be in!

'I didn't bring one.' And, at her slight groan, 'Do not worry, I was wearing a robe. It is somewhere down there.' He pointed to the shadowy tables and chairs at the far end of the pool. 'I can look for it, if you like?'

'I'll get it.' She leant over the pool and handed him her towel as she added, 'Dry yourself off with this while I get the robe and wrap it round yourself.' Please. *Please*.

She didn't stop to see if he obeyed her or not, she simply scuttled off into the shadows, her eyes searching for the robe. She found it almost immediately lying on a chair but waited for a good couple of minutes before she turned round and retraced her steps. A football team could have dried themselves in the time.

Andreas was sitting on a chair by the pool, the towel wrapped low around his lean hips and his long muscled legs stretched out in front of him. He was the epitome of the relaxed male, his face open and innocent as she approached. 'Great, you've found it,' he said approvingly, and then, as she shivered, added, 'You're cold, Sophy. Put it on; I don't need it.'

Put it on? His robe? The robe that had his very definite male smell all about it and seemed an extension of the man himself? Was he mad? And her shiver hadn't been due to cold—far from it. She caught his eyes wandering over her breasts, their tips hard and pointed as they thrust against the wet black silk, and she folded her arms as casually as she could as she said, 'I'm fine, thanks. Keep the towel and leave it outside my door in the morning. I'm just going back to the—'

'Sit down, Sophy. We need to talk,' he interrupted her easily.

'Andreas, it's the middle of the night.'

'All the better for what I need to say,' he returned coolly.

'I don't think—'

'For crying out loud, woman!' He rose in one swift movement that made her fear for the towel, taking the robe from her suddenly numb fingers and wrapping it round her before she could protest. 'Now sit down and listen, will you?' he said a trifle irritably. 'I need to talk to you about

Theodore. That is one of the reasons—the main reason—I stayed on tonight. My father feels it is only fair to acquaint Jill with the full facts but he and my mother find it difficult to talk about this, for reasons which will become clear to you. He has therefore asked me to explain. I was going to ask to see you both tomorrow morning before I left for the office, but perhaps it is better to tell you informally like this and then you can explain in your own words to Jill.'

She stared at him as she sank down on to the seat he indicated, aware that this must be something very serious from his tense expression but finding it difficult to concentrate on anything at all with the lemony masculine fragrance of him all about her. But the robe *was* warm and the night air distinctly nippy, she told herself silently, ignoring the tingling heat that was spreading through her and which had nothing to do with the texture of the material and all to do with Andreas Karydis.

Andreas sat down again, pulling the towel tighter round his thighs—for which small mercy Sophy was very grateful—and then remained looking at her for a moment or two without speaking.

The shadowed darkness was quite silent, apart from the odd call from the numerous insects and night-life in the vegetation surrounding the pool, and the scent of magnolia was heavy on the air when at last Andreas began to speak.

'You have to understand what I am going to tell you from a background of the Greek way of life,' Andreas said quietly. 'And especially how it was some forty or fifty years ago. It was a man's world, then; maybe it still is, especially in the smaller villages where the family is very patriarchal and a woman's role is very clearly defined. My mother was born in just such a village, a fishing village far away from here in the south.'

He paused, looking away from her and across the pool, and Sophy realised he was finding this very hard. 'Andreas, you really don't have to explain anything,' she said quickly, negating everything she had thought earlier in the house.

'Unfortunately, that is not so,' he contradicted quietly. 'My father has asked me to tell you it all. Jill is Theodore's wife and there can be no secrets within the family, although it is up to her exactly what she tells her son.'

He paused again, and then said, 'My mother is a very beautiful woman even now; when she was younger she was quite exceptionally lovely. In the village where she lived there was a man. He wanted her but she did not want him, so in order to make sure she married him he waited his opportunity and, when she was separated from her friends one night, he raped her. She was fifteen years old.'

'Oh, Andreas.' Whatever she had expected it wasn't this and her shocked face spoke for itself.

'This man had two fishing boats and was considered good husband material by my mother's family. When he went to my mother's father and told him what he had done—my mother had been too ashamed to tell anyone—it was agreed he would marry her immediately. The shame, you see, was all on my mother's side, according to her family; this man was just acting as a man must.'

The bitterness was tangible and now Sophy didn't say a word, but she realised that in the telling of his mother's story she was seeing a side to this big, ruthless, hard individual she hadn't realised existed. A tender, softer side that could feel hurt.

'The day after the marriage had been agreed, a storm sprang up whilst the fishing boats were out. Two were lost. This man was on one of them. My mother was glad he had died—she hated him—but a few weeks later she realised he had not left her after all; his seed had taken root and was growing inside her.'

'Theodore?' Sophy whispered in horror, drawing the folds of the robe more closely around her.

'Yes, Theodore, my big brother,' Andreas said so harshly she winced. 'It was three years before my father's yacht made an unscheduled stop at the village harbour one evening, three years of hell for my mother at the hands of her so-called family and neighbours. She was made to suffer in a hundred different ways for the ''sin'' she had committed.'

He drew in a deep breath and when he spoke again he had control of his voice. 'My father's yacht had engine trouble and he noticed my mother helping pack fish from the night's catch. Without a man of her own, she was expected to do most things herself. For my father it was love at first sight and he did not rest until he had persuaded her to marry him and leave all the past behind her—except Theodore, of course. She loved her son in spite of the way he had been conceived. And so he brought her and the boy north—he was rich enough to buy her a new beginning in a place where she was respected as his wife—and brought up Theodore as his own son.'

'And he found out,' Sophy said half to herself, the heady sweet smell of the magnolia flowers suddenly a mockery in view of the painful story she was hearing. 'Theodore found out.'

'Yes, he found out,' Andreas said flatly, 'and, being his father's son, he vented his spleen on my mother. You think I am unfair?' he added tightly as she looked at him with wide eyes. 'I am not, Sophy. We never got on, I and Theodore, and when I was informed of the reason he had taken off for England I could see why. His father's blood ran hot and strong in his veins. He was an aggressive youth, given to fits of temper and with a streak of pure malice for those who crossed him. Maybe those first three years stayed somewhere in his subconscious, I don't know, but he was fiercely proud and possessive.'

'He blamed Dimitra?'

'Oh, yes, and one night he and my father rowed violently and came to blows. My mother tried to separate them and he said the most unforgivable things to her; she has never been the same since. In spite of everything she had gone through before she married my father she had never been crushed, not until that night. My father gave Theodore a sum of money, enough to start the restaurant business in England and so on, and Theodore left with my mother's pleas for him to forgive her ringing in his ears. *Forgive her!* Her! He was not worthy to lick her boots.'

'I'm sorry, Andreas. I don't know what to say.'

'You did not like him, did you, Sophy? You could not have liked him,' he said in response to her soft, shocked voice.

He was looking straight into her eyes now and for a moment the virile masculinity that was an essential part of him made her breathless. 'No, I didn't like him,' she agreed faintly.

'I have thanked God there is nothing of Theodore in his son,' Andreas said grimly. 'When I first saw the boy it was a shock; he is the physical image of his father, but that is all. Here inside, where it counts, Michael is free of the curse.'

He had placed his clenched fist on his chest as he spoke and as her eyes followed the gesture the maleness of him was again paramount. She shivered slightly, pulling the robe closer.

'You might think me hard towards my own brother,' Andreas said very quietly, 'but I learnt as a young child you do not extend the hand of love and comradeship to a rabid dog unless you want it bitten off. We never liked each other; long before Theodore discovered his parentage this was so. Part of his fury when he found out he was not my father's son was that he felt I had taken his place within the family.'

Sophy could find it within herself to feel sorry for Theodore but she was wise enough not to say so. Whatever Jill's husband had said and done before he had left his homeland had affected Dimitra badly, and it was clear Andreas would never forgive his half-sibling for the agony and grief he had caused their mother.

'Theodore said—' She stopped abruptly, not sure if she should go on—whether it was the right time to ask questions.

'Yes?' Andreas said a touch impatiently. 'What did he say?'

'He said the family cut him off for good when he married Jill,' Sophy said hesitantly. 'Obviously you'd all quarrelled before then, but he insinuated to Jill that his marriage was the final straw as far as his family in Greece was concerned.'

'That is not true.' Glittering grey eyes searched her face grimly. 'You have seen my mother, Sophy; do you really think she is capable of such bigotry? And my father worships the ground she walks on; he would have done anything to heal the breach between Theodore and my mother. For himself...' Andreas paused before continuing, 'I will not lie to you; he was bitterly angry with Theodore's attitude towards her, and his feelings are the same as mine, but neither of us have betrayed this to my mother. Theodore made her very ill—she had a nervous breakdown with the strain of it all after he had gone to England. My father could never have forgotten this if Theodore had lived, not even if the future had brought some kind of reconciliation.'

He had talked of Theodore being proud and unforgiving but Andreas and his father were just the same, Sophy thought. And then a little voice in her head said, But their attitude had been formed through love for Dimitra and what Theodore had done to her, whereas Theodore's stance had been taken through hate.

Was she making excuses for Andreas? The thought shocked her, intimating, as it did, that she wanted to think the best of him. Which was ridiculous considering the way they had been at each other's throats from the first moment they had laid eyes on one another. But he wasn't quite what she'd thought he was.

Sophy didn't like the way her thoughts were going and now said quickly, 'I believe you, of course I believe you. Dimitra is so sweet. She couldn't possibly have treated Theodore badly.'

'She is a wonderful woman,' he agreed quietly.

Andreas's voice unconsciously gentled when he spoke of his mother, Sophy noticed, and she had observed earlier the way he and Evangelos treated Dimitra like precious, rare porcelain. It must be nice to be adored by two such strong, powerful men; one a devoted husband and the other a loving son.

Again she drew her mind away from the path it was following, saying softly, 'Thank you for telling me all this, Andreas, and I'll make sure Jill understands how things are. I'm sure she won't find it necessary to tell Michael anything now or in the future; it's probably best he remembers his father the way he does now, which is as a remote figure on the perimeter of his life. Michael actually gets on better with Christos, Theodore's partner in the restaurant, than he ever did his father.'

Andreas nodded slowly. 'My father has been in communication with Christos and he has appreciated the man's tact and genuine consideration. It is good Jill has someone like him in the business.'

His face was closed and grim; he obviously had not liked having to reveal such intimate facts about his parents to a virtual stranger but it was hardly her fault, Sophy thought, before she warned herself not to be so touchy. She wasn't normally like this—but then, since she had met Andreas, she was beginning to realise there were things about herself of which she had had no idea. And she didn't like that.

She swallowed hard. 'I'd better get back,' she said awkwardly, rising to her feet with the robe still held tightly round her. She thought about offering it back but as it was quite on the cards for Andreas to pass her the towel if she did, she decided against it.

He had risen when she did and she found it incredibly difficult to concentrate on anything but the powerfully muscled body in front of her, hearing him say, 'I hope once these distressing matters are out of the way you and your sister and Michael will enjoy your stay in my beautiful country,' through hot prickles of rising sensation.

It seemed particularly ironic that the most civilised conversation they had had to date was being conducted with Andreas all but naked and she enveloped in his bath robe. She took a deep breath and managed a somewhat shaky, 'Thank you.'

His voice had been dark and smoky and his face wasn't grim any more; in fact, it was wearing an expression she hadn't seen before and it turned her limbs fluid. 'Do I frighten you, Sophy? Do you still see me as a threat?' he asked softly as her heartbeats accelerated to a hundred miles per hour.

'Of course not.' She tried for briskness but failed miserably. 'And I didn't see you as a threat exactly,' she lied firmly.

'Good.' He smiled, a slow, sexy smile and Sophy knew she ought to get the hell out of there but she was unable to move.

His eyes were as black as midnight and they held her wide blue ones with no effort at all, her lids falling half shut as his face came closer and his firm warm lips met hers in a light, almost teasing kiss. He drew her against his firm hard flesh, one arm round the small of her back as his other hand tilted her chin for greater access to her mouth.

He smelt of the cold, clean water and the night, and as her head began to spin the kiss deepened beyond the soft coaxing he'd employed at first. His lips and tongue were sensuous and experienced but he didn't rush her, his control enormous, as he pleasured them both.

Her hands were grasping the hard muscled flesh of his broad shoulders, although she had no recollection of how they got there and, although she was pressed so close to him now that she could feel the effect her body was having on his, she could no more have drawn away than flown to the moon.

He was kissing her deeply and slowly, building sensation upon sensation, and nothing in the world could have stopped Sophy from kissing him back. The hard pressure of his hair-roughened chest as he crushed her against him, the sensuous quality of his mouth, the overriding authority and power as he took the sweetness from her mouth with no consideration that she might refuse him was intoxicating. She couldn't believe how intoxicating.

She had never been kissed like this, never had such overwhelming sensations tearing through her flesh and making her moist and feverish in a man's arms. She felt as though she was on fire and he seemed to know just what to do to make the flames burn more fiercely.

There was a tight ache in her breasts, their peaks sharply tender, and it was bewildering because suddenly her body wasn't her own. She had always assumed she must have a low sex drive because Matthew's desire to only make love once every four or five weeks had never bothered her unduly. Their union had been comforting and reassuring rather than anything else, a relaxing and almost homely reinforcement of their friendship and high regard for each other. As had breakfast in bed on a Sunday and walks in the park.

But this, this took away her will and reason, shooting sensations to parts of her body she had never been aware of before. It made her want more, much more—made her dangerously out of control. The warning registered in her brain with enough force to cause Sophy to jerk back away from the warmth of him with a little cry of distress, the knowledge that she had been in danger of casting off every rule and principle she had lived by for the last twenty-eight years enough to bring her back to reality.

'Don't touch me!' Her voice was high and frantic, and through the rushing shame and humiliation that was pounding in her head a tiny part of her mind registered he obeyed instantly, even though his eyes were hungry and his muscled body taut and hard with passion. 'I don't want this! This is not why I stayed down here. You asked me to listen about Theodore, that's all.'

She was crying out against herself as much as him, against the insanity that had allowed her to lose all rhyme and reason the minute he had touched her. It was crazy, unthinkable—what she had nearly allowed. And with Andreas Karydis. *Andreas Karydis* of all people! She had only met him a few hours ago.

'Sophy, listen to me—'

'No, don't you dare come near me!' And then, in her panic and confusion, she said something unforgivable before she ran from him. 'You're just like them! Theodore and his father! Forcing yourself on women to get what you want.'

And then she was running from him, the robe slipping from her arms and falling on the ground as she sped across the cool tiles and then out on to the soft velvety grass beyond, careless of the clothes she had left behind as she ran as though the devil himself was at her heels. Which was exactly how she felt.

By the time she reached the sanctuary of her room, her breath was sobbing in her throat and the realisation was dawning that she had made a monumental fool of herself. She sank down on the bed, shaking uncontrollably as she relived the last few seconds with Andreas and what she had screamed at him. How could she? How *could* she have said he was like his brother and that madman who had sired Theodore? What a terrible thing to have thrown in his face.

She sat, shivering and shaking on the edge of the bed as she went over and over in her mind what had occurred, before she threw herself face down on the covers and cried her eyes out. A good ten minutes later, when her face was red and blotchy and her eyes so swollen she felt she was peering through two slits, she forced herself to emerge from the deep well of despair.

She would have to apologise to him for that last remark. The knowledge was like a hard lead ball in the pit of her stomach. It had been nasty and cruel, and most of all it hadn't been true. She had wanted what had happened just as much as he had, if not more. She groaned softly at her weakness, hating herself.

He was clearly the playboy type, or perhaps work hard and play hard was a more accurate description, but whatever—she had been nothing more than a brief dalliance as far as he was concerned. And she'd offered herself on a plate, after all.

Andreas was fabulously wealthy with the sort of personal charisma which would ensure the women were lining up in their droves. No doubt he only had to crook his little finger and a queue formed—and she'd fallen straight into line. No different to all the rest. Thank you very much for noticing me, Mr Karydis, and of course I'll keep your bed warm. *Idiot!* She gritted her teeth against the mental self-flagellation. Idiot, idiot, idiot! She had deserved exactly what she had got.

She should have listened quietly to his explanation for the split within his family; offered her condolences and reassurances that Jill wouldn't rock the Karydis boat; and exited gracefully. Instead— She bit her lip until she felt the salty taste of blood. Instead she had responded like a nymphomaniac to what he had probably intended as a brief goodnight kiss, and then accused him of intended rape. Virtually. Oh, what a mess.

She groaned softly, running her hand through her hair distractedly before sitting up and then sliding off the bed. A long, cool shower was a must and then she would lie down with a cold flannel across her swollen eyes. The family would think she had gone a few rounds with a boxer if she walked down to breakfast like this tomorrow.

She knew she had a reputation within the fashion fraternity of being icy cool and formidably in control of herself, and it was an image she had deliberately fostered during the last years. So what had happened in the last twenty-four hours?

Andreas Karydis had happened. It was stark and distinctly unsavoury, but it was the truth.

She chewed everything over whilst under the shower, and by the time she was tucked up in bed—the cold flannel in place and the light silky covers up to her chin—she had come to a decision. Tomorrow she would phone her secretary, Annie, and tell her to call the Karydis residence during the afternoon indicating Sophy's immediate presence was required back in London.

Okay, so it was sneaky, but she had seen enough of Dimitra and Evangelos to know that Jill and Michael were amongst friends here, and she could keep in contact by telephone with Jill and make sure everything went smoothly for her sister. She had never done anything like this before in her life but extreme circumstances called for extreme measures, and if ever a situation was extreme this one was. She needed to put as much space between herself and Andreas Karydis as possible, and if it felt like running away or ducking out of her responsibilities then that was tough—better that than staying. Oh, yes, indubitably.

Decision made, she was asleep in thirty seconds, utterly worn out by all the emotional turmoil.

CHAPTER FIVE

SOPHY awoke the next morning to a gentle hand touching her forehead and Jill's concerned voice saying, 'Oh, Sophy, is your head no better? You should have said you felt so rotten. I didn't realise. Can I get you some aspirin or something?'

The flannel was still across her face, dried now but providing silent but eloquent justification for her swollen eyelids, and as Sophy sat up and put it to one side she knew she looked pretty bad from the way Jill stared at her. Guilt led her to say quickly, 'I'm fine now, Jill, really. It was just one of those headache things caused by the flight and the heat, no doubt. I'll have a shower and then come down with you to breakfast, shall I?'

'Breakfast's over; it's gone ten.' Jill pointed to the bright sunshine outside the window. 'I've brought you a tray Christina prepared for you, but there's no rush to get up. Have the morning in bed if you want. Evangelos and Andreas have gone into the office and Dimitra has taken Michael for a walk round the estate, so it's just the two of us for a while.'

'Right.' Andreas's name had brought a flood of colour into her face and Sophy quickly bent forwards, allowing the silky veil of her hair to hide her hot cheeks as she pretended to straighten the bedclothes. How she was going to face him again she didn't know.

'Isn't it just beautiful here?' Jill placed the tray containing warm, freshly baked croissants and preserves, fresh fruit and orange juice on her sister's lap, before strolling across the room and opening the glass doors leading on to the balcony so that the fresh, richly scented sunshine spilled into the room. 'I can't imagine what would drive Theodore to leave all this, can you? And Dimitra and Evangelos are so *nice*, Andreas too, although you'd hardly think he and Theodore were brothers.'

Sophy's silence must have spoken for itself, because Jill turned round and looked at her twin before saying tentatively, 'What? What is it?' as she saw the look on her sister's face.

'Come and sit down. I've got something to tell you,' Sophy said quietly. 'Or, better still, I'll join you on the balcony and we can sit in the sunshine while we talk.'

She related her conversation with Andreas almost word for word, and when she had finished speaking Jill remained staring out over the beautiful grounds bathed in brilliant sunshine for some moments before she said, 'It explains a lot.'

'I guess it does,' Sophy said quietly.

'Certainly why Theodore was so difficult to live with, even how we came to be married. He was obsessional about me from the first time he saw me, like his father seems to have been about Dimitra. I was flattered at first, I suppose, to have someone so crazy about me and I did love him then, in the early days.'

'And later?' Sophy asked very softly.

'He frightened me,' Jill admitted quietly as she turned to look straight into Sophy's blue eyes. 'He only wanted me to see him, think about him, talk to him. I…even think he was jealous of Michael because it took some of my attention away from him. He…he had these jealous rages if I even talked to someone on the telephone too long, and when he was like that there was no reasoning with him. Michael learnt to stay out of his way.'

'Was he violent?' Sophy sensed there was much more Jill wasn't saying. 'Physically violent, I mean?'

'Not at first, but after Michael was born…' Jill shrugged. 'I was careful to say and do nothing to upset him in the end.'

It was all Sophy's worst fears come true, and she stared at Jill's dear face before saying quietly, 'Why didn't you leave him, Jill? Or tell someone about it? Me, at least.'

'He would never have let me go,' Jill said flatly, 'and if I had attempted to leave him it would have ended in tragedy. You didn't know him, Sophy. As for why I didn't say anything…' She turned to look over the gardens again. 'Many reasons, I guess, but the main one was that I knew it wouldn't do any good and might do a lot of harm if he found out. You see, I'm not like you—I'm not a fighter. I never have been.'

'I wouldn't say I'm a fighter,' Sophy said in surprise.

'Well, you are.' Jill smiled sadly. 'Which is why Theodore didn't like you. He knew you would have rocked the boat and kept rocking it until he fell out!'

'Oh, Jill.' Sophy reached across and hugged her sister. 'I'm so sorry for the way your marriage turned out, but at least you've got Michael. He's a wonderful little boy.'

'And he makes every moment, good and bad, of the last seven years worthwhile,' Jill agreed warmly. 'A hundred times over.'

They talked some more before Jill wandered off to find Dimitra and Michael whilst Sophy got bathed and dressed, but long after Jill had left Sophy continued to sit in the sunshine. Her eyes were fixed on a mass of oleanders in the distance, the rich green clusters of foliage crowned with bursts of pink and white flowers quite beautiful, but Sophy wasn't really seeing them at all. Her vision was all within herself.

Would she ever have children? she asked herself silently, the conversation with Jill having sparked off a vague feeling of depression. She couldn't imagine going through life

childless, and yet she had never really seen herself and
Matthew in a family setting somehow. She had heard
women remark that they were longing to have their partner's baby, but she'd never felt like that about Matthew.
Was that wrong?

But Matthew had always been ill at ease with children,
she reminded herself in the next moment, and the fragility
of babies had frankly horrified him. When one of their close
friends had asked him to be godfather to their first-born he
had refused point blank, deeply offending the couple in
question.

Now, in spite of Andreas's big, powerful build and aggressively masculine demeanour, she could picture him cra-
dling an infant with the utmost tenderness, and his easy
rapport with Michael had been immediate. He would be a
natural as a father. Andreas Karydis as a father holding his
newborn baby... Making babies with Andreas Karydis...

The harsh jarring call of what sounded like a peacock
somewhere outside the confines of the grounds brought
Sophy back to earth with a bump, and when she realised
what she had been daydreaming about she went hot with
mortification.

She was losing it, she really was! She'd be a candidate
for the funny farm at this rate. She didn't know what had
happened to her from the minute she had stepped foot in
this country but she didn't like it one little bit!

She jumped up from the chair and stalked into the bedroom, her face set. But one thing had changed this morning;
she was darned if she was going to high-tail it back to
England like a little scared rabbit. Jill had called her a
fighter and maybe she was at that, because now, in the cold
clear light of day, the thought of running away was just not
an option. She hadn't been herself last night—not in any
way, shape or form—but that was last night and today was
today and things were going to be different.

Andreas Karydis was just a man like any other; she had blown this whole thing up into something it wasn't. When she saw him again—*if* she saw him again—she would offer a cool apology for her last words to him the night before, at the same time as making it perfectly clear she had no intention of being so foolish as to repeat the exercise that prompted her outburst. Simple, she assured herself as she began to run a warm bath. No need for dramatics or rushing off home to England or anything else. She was a mature and competent woman who could deal with any hiccup life chose to inflict on her. Andreas might be rather a large hiccup, but a hiccup he was, nevertheless.

The three women and Michael spent a lazy afternoon by the pool after a light alfresco lunch. Jill and Dimitra insisted on it, declaring Sophy must take it easy after such a bad headache the night before. Their concern made her feel horribly guilty but Michael's transparent joy at being able to hop in and out of the pool all day eased her sore conscience a little. The small boy was clearly having a whale of a time and was already turning nut brown, although Jill and Sophy spent most of their time under the shade of the trees at the far end of the pool, mindful of the effect of the burning sun on their pale English skin.

After a couple of dips in the pool Sophy changed into a thin white cotton shirt top and long matching skirt, mid-afternoon. In spite of staying out of the sun her skin was turning rosy pink and she used that as an excuse to cover up. In actual fact, it was more the fact that Andreas might— just might—call by before returning to his own home, and if that happened she wanted—needed—to be as different from the girl he had met by the pool in the darkness of night as it was possible to be.

She lay on one of the loungers, the dark shade broken into patches by dappled sunlight, and idly watched Dimitra playing with Michael in the shallow end of the pool; Jill was fast asleep on another lounger at the side of her.

She wasn't aware of shutting her eyes, but the few hours of fragmented rest she had managed the night before must have caught up with her, because when she surfaced from a deep sleep it was to the realisation that the sun was no longer high in a blue sky but falling softly into the shadows of evening, and Andreas had taken Jill's place on the lounger beside her.

There was no smile on Andreas's face as he watched her eyes slowly focus and then widen as she sat up abruptly, and his handsome face was cold and still as she stuttered, 'I...I must have fallen asleep. What—where are Jill and Michael?'

'It is seven o'clock. Michael has had his tea and his mother is getting him ready for bed.'

There was a brooding quality to his presence and he looked devastatingly foreign, his formal shirt and loose tie, along with his suit trousers, indicating he was still in his office attire. The collar of his shirt was undone and revealed his bronzed muscled neck, and she noticed his eyes were so dark a grey as to be black, with a glittering fire in them that spoke of some emotion. Anger at her, no doubt, after last night.

She didn't stop to think, she just said, 'I want to apologise for what I said last night, Andreas. It was unfair and untrue. You aren't a bit like Theodore.'

He said nothing at all for a moment, and then moved in his seat, leaning back and stretching his long legs. 'Thank you. I won't argue with you.'

There was more than a touch of dryness in his voice but Sophy was relieved he hadn't been more difficult. 'Last night—' she waved what she hoped he perceived as a casual hand '—I was overtired and not thinking straight.'

'I see.' He let his dark gaze run over her soft blonde hair

and creamy, sunkissed skin, and she found herself flushing scarlet in spite of all her efforts to appear nonchalant and in control.

'I was not overtired and there was nothing wrong with my thinking,' he drawled with silky composure. 'I wanted to kiss you; I had been wondering what you tasted like from the first moment I saw you at the airport.'

She stared at him, immediately on the defensive. 'Look, Andreas, I'm here to keep Jill company, that's all,' she said quickly, relieved her voice sounded more firm than she expected.

He gave her a hard look. 'Do I take it you are informing me there will be no repeat of last night?' he asked expressionlessly.

'Exactly. I'm sorry.' She was relieved it had been so easy.

His frown changed to a quizzical ruffle which did the most peculiar things to her nerve endings. 'You're not at all sorry,' he said mildly. 'Right from the first you have been fighting me, have you not?'

First Jill, now him. Had she got 'fighter' tattooed on her forehead or something? 'Not at all,' she said carefully. 'I admit we haven't hit it off, though, but that's life.'

'The hell we haven't.' He straightened in the chair and she had to force her body not to react. 'Don't you recognise sexual chemistry when you feel it? The issue here is not that we haven't hit it off, Sophy, but that we've hit it off too fiercely for your mind to cope with. Your body, however, knows exactly what it wants.'

She couldn't believe he was sitting there saying these things to her with such a matter-of-fact tone of voice. She glared at him, her body stiff and tense and her face expressing her outrage. 'That's ridiculous,' she said icily. 'And you know it.'

He refused to accept her self-denial. 'No, it's the truth whether you like it or not.'

'I don't like it,' she shot back tightly. 'Neither do I appreciate the fact that you obviously think I'm the sort of woman who sleeps around.'

'You think because I kissed you I assume you sleep around?' Andreas said incredulously.

'No. Yes. I mean—' He was tying her up in knots! 'I don't wish to discuss this,' she said hotly, drawing the tattered remains of her dignity about her as she rose to her feet. 'I'm going to get ready for dinner. Goodbye, Andreas.'

'I've been invited to stay for dinner,' he said with suspicious meekness. 'Is that all right with you?'

'This is your parents's home,' she said primly. 'I wouldn't dream of suggesting you shouldn't stay. You must do as you please.'

'Thank you, Sophy.' He eyed her with barely concealed amusement.

He had risen with her, and now, as she felt his hand at her elbow, she drew in a deep breath and forced herself to show no reaction at all to his touch as they began walking back towards the house, even though she could feel the vitality and strength that was such an essential part of him flowing through his fingertips and making her flesh tingle. She wanted to shrug his hand away but it would be too crass, and so she concentrated on putting one foot in front of the other and ignored what the touch of his thigh against hers was doing to her equilibrium.

'Your clothes are in my car,' he said softly without looking at her as they walked. 'I didn't think it wise to leave them down by the pool as it might have prompted a question or two in view of your early departure after dinner, but I thought if I returned them to you last night it might have…disturbed you.'

Huh! She could hear the hidden laughter in his voice and her face was straight when she said tightly, 'Thank you.'

'My pleasure,' he returned smoothly. 'And I shall leave for my own home straight after dinner so if you feel inclined for another midnight dip, please do not hesitate on my account.'

'I won't,' she assured him with a tartness that made the dark eyebrows rise just a fraction in silent reproach.

For all the world as though he didn't know he had been deliberately goading her, she told herself savagely. But he had known all right. He was just loving this, all of it. But at least his quiet mockery sent hot pride flooding into every nerve and sinew and enabled her to march back to the house with her head held high and her back straight.

Sophy was applying the last light touch of make-up to her flawless skin before joining the others downstairs when the knock sounded at her door. Jill had already gone down some minutes earlier when Sophy had urged her to do so after her sister had knocked on her door, and Sophy had been pleased Jill had appeared quite happy to do so. Jill's confidence was definitely improving.

Thinking her sister had come to hurry her, she called out gaily, 'All right, all right, I'm ready, don't worry!' as she rose and walked to the door.

Andreas was leaning lazily against the opposite wall when she opened the door, and in spite of the fact that the previous night had prepared her for what the sight of the big, lean body encased in an immaculate dinner suit did to her senses, she found she had to take a breath or two before she could say, 'Oh I'm sorry, I thought you were Jill, come to tell me I'm taking too long,' as her cheeks began to burn with annoying colour.

'Take as long as you like.' He levered himself away and

reached for the small bag at his feet. 'Your clothes,' he offered imperturbably, his expression definitely sardonic.

His bronzed skin and black hair seemed ever darker against the light cream wall. He looked all male, the veneer of civilisation barely held in check. She caught the fanciful thought, angry with herself but shivering without knowing why.

'Thank you; I'm ready now.' She took the bag and walked across to place it on a chair, and when she turned back Andreas was framed in the doorway. His grey eyes lingered for a moment on the pure honey-tinted curve of her throat as she stood, slim and ethereal in the pale blue silk cocktail dress she had chosen to wear, and something in his gaze made her voice slightly breathless as she said, 'Won't it look a little strange if we go downstairs together? I'll wait a moment or two, if you like.'

'I don't like.' His voice was not hostile; rather, it had that thick smoky edge which had haunted her dreams the night before.

'But they might wonder—'

'Sophy, my parents and Jill have more important things to do than to wonder at the incredible sight of two people walking into the dining room together,' he said matter of factly, the sheer patience in his voice emphasising how silly she was being.

She nodded jerkily, wondering how it was that Andreas always made her feel like she was eighteen instead of twenty-eight, or perhaps a young gauche girl just entering her teens was more apt. Her normal cool common sense seemed to take one look at him and fly out of the window. Still, she was the only person who could change that so she'd better pull herself together. Right now.

She picked up the small silk purse in the exact shade of the dress and joined him on the landing, brushing past him as he stood aside for her to exit but with his hand still holding the door.

The contact, brief though it had been, brought a hectic pink flush to her cheeks as they walked along the corridor towards the stairs, but if Andreas noticed he didn't comment.

As they walked together down the wide staircase, Sophy slanted a surreptitious glance at him from the corner of her eye. The hard profile was giving nothing away. The strong forehead, black brows, straight thin nose and square chin could have been sculpted in granite for all the expression they held.

Sophy swallowed drily as her eyes rested a moment more on his firm, nicely moulded mouth before she dragged her gaze away. The memory of that kiss had been with her all day; even when it hadn't been in the forefront of her mind it had been lurking in her subconscious. She hated it but she didn't seem to be able to help it.

She could still feel how it had felt to be held so close to that big rugged body; even now her flesh was tingling at his closeness whereas he— She bit her lip hard as a mixture of self-disgust and irritation made her soft mouth tighten. He seemed quite oblivious to her supposed charms. And yet he had admitted down by the pool earlier that he felt the sexual chemistry between them every little bit as much as she did.

So what did that mean? That he could control himself better than she could? That thought wasn't to be borne, and it brought her sweeping ahead of him into the dining room with her backbone rigid and her eyes narrowed. She just had time to compose her face into a more socially acceptable expression before the others turned from where they were standing on the patio and called for Andreas and Sophy to join them.

The meal was as good as the night before and the conversation even better now Jill had gained enough confidence to do her part. Christina was a first-class cook and fiercely Greek, which meant most of the delicious dishes paraded in front of her Sophy hadn't tried before, but every one was excellent. Dolmades—meat and rice wrapped in vine leaves—and taramasalata—a compote of fish roes, garlic and lemon leavened by breadcrumbs—were two of Christina's staple dishes, but the table groaned with other succulent morsels.

Fried potatoes, slices of eggplant in batter, olives, cheeses, bowls of tomato, cucumber and peppers, seafood in various disguises, meatballs in thick sauce, plates of cold sliced veal, pork and lamb were all brought in at various stages of the long, leisurely meal. Sophy found souvlak—a pancake of brown meal garnished with tomatoes, peppers, onions and yoghurt and filled with thin slices of lean meat which had been pressed into a cone and cooked over a grill—to be especially to her liking, but it was all delicious. And Dimitra explained each dish in her soft gentle voice, giving a list of the ingredients and its Greek name along with the way they were cooked.

Evangelos's specialty was the wine, and at least three different varieties of both white and red had been brought out by the time the coffee and ouzo appeared.

It was an amazing lifestyle, Sophy thought, as she glanced round the beautifully decorated room beyond which the lights on the patio showed the gardens stretching away into the dusky night. Incredibly luxurious and opulent, and yet all the money in the world hadn't enabled Evangelos to do the one thing he had wanted with all his heart—to protect the woman he loved from further hurt in her life.

He had brought her out of the shame and misery which had been thrust upon her, provided the ivory palace of fairytale stories and more or less wrapped Dimitra up in cotton wool, but still the older woman had suffered to the point where her mental health had been broken when Theodore had rejected her so cruelly. And it had been cruel, wickedly cruel. She couldn't see Andreas treating his mother so badly, whatever the circumstances.

Immediately the thought materialised, the warning bells were clanging. What did she know about Andreas? Nothing at all beyond the fact that at times he could be just as hard and uncompromising as Theodore had been, so he might be quite capable of hurting Dimitra. Whatever, it was none of her business. This family was nothing to her beyond Jill's involvement with them. The old feud with its ongoing ramifications, along with the lives of Andreas and his parents, would soon be a distant memory once she was back in England; two weeks was just a brief flash of time in the overall span of things.

The air was heavier and more humid than it had been the night before, and when Dimitra suggested that they take their coffee on the patio to benefit from any slight breeze everyone agreed. Sophy especially was longing for a change of scene.

It was a little cooler outside and almost dark, the night sky of dark charcoal streaked with bands of silver grey and dull mauve. The scent of the climbing roses which twined all over the back of the house was rich and sweet in the warm air, and Sophy found her taut nerves were beginning to relax a little as she sat and sipped her coffee and listened to the others chat.

Christina had just bustled in and poured the women another coffee when Jill said, 'I think I'll just go and check on Michael before I drink mine,' turning to Dimitra as she finished and adding, 'Would you like to come with me?' Dimitra had apparently accompanied her daughter-in-law the night before when Jill had looked in on her son before retiring, and it had touched Jill how Dimitra had stood for ages just watching her grandson sleep.

As the two women stood up, Evangelos also rose, saying in an aside to Andreas, 'I'll make that telephone call to Athos to confirm the shipping dates now. I won't be long,' and before Sophy could blink she found herself alone with Andreas in the warm scented night.

She wasn't aware she had shifted uneasily until the smoky voice at her elbow said softly, 'Relax, Sophy. I'm not about to leap on you if that's what you are thinking.'

She made the mistake of turning to look him full in the face, and the dark sardonic gleam in the grey eyes informed her all too clearly he was loving her confusion.

'Don't be ridiculous,' she said stiffly, wishing she could think of a crushing retort to put him in his place.

'A kiss. I am to be hung, drawn and quartered for a kiss. Is that it?' he asked very quietly.

Put like that it sounded nothing, she admitted silently, but she knew—as well as Andreas did—that something vital and electric had leapt into being between them the moment his lips had touched hers. And if she hadn't called a halt, who knew what might have occurred in the perfumed darkness by the pool?

'You are determined not to mellow an inch, are you not? I am cast into the role of wicked philanderer and this will make it easier for you to ignore the truth,' he stated flatly.

'The truth?' she asked warily, wondering what was coming.

'The truth your body recognised from the first moment we met—that we are compatible sexually in a way that happens with few couples.' He looked at her, daring her to deny it.

'We're not a couple,' she pointed out swiftly, hot colour burning her cheeks, 'and you can't possibly say that, considering we've never even—' she paused for the briefest of moments before finishing '—slept together.'

'I am more than willing to put my theory to the test,' Andreas offered helpfully, leaning back in his chair as he crossed one knee over the other and surveyed her from laughing grey eyes, his face remaining completely serious.

Sophy gritted her teeth. 'How kind, but if you don't mind I'll decline your generous offer.'

He grinned openly then and she didn't like the rush of sensation that almost overwhelmed her as the hard, handsome face relaxed and softened.

He had slid into the seat Dimitra had vacated as the others had left, and now he stared at her for a moment before saying softly, the amusement dying from his face, 'You have the most beautiful eyes, do you know that? And they are a deeper violet than Jill's. Your hair is different too. Yours is a little paler than Jill's, silver almost, like moonlit water. You really are not so alike after all.'

He was close enough for her to be wrapped up in his male aura and it took a second for her to be able to say, her voice striving for lightness, 'There is no danger of mistaking us then?' as she tried to wrench her gaze from his.

'None at all.' He took one of her hands as though he had the right to do so, and when she instinctively tried to pull it away secured her fingers in one hand with her palm uppermost as his other hand casually stroked the soft full flesh. 'Soft and silky,' he murmured almost to himself, 'such fine transparent skin.' And then he had raised her palm to his lips, touching her flesh gently just for a moment.

A tingle shot straight up her arm and this time when she pulled away he let her go, settling back in Dimitra's chair more comfortably as his eyes narrowed on her flushed face. He folded his arms over his chest, and then said evenly, as though the rest of their conversation hadn't happened,

'Come out to dinner with me tomorrow night, just the two of us. I know a little place you would love down by the seafront.'

Was he mad? Sophy placed her hands in her lap and stared at him through the whirling in her head. 'No, thank you.'

'Why not?' he responded immediately.

He knew darn well why not! 'I don't want to,' she said ungraciously. 'Okay?' She eyed him defiantly.

'That's not an answer. Give me a reason. Is it because you are frightened to be alone with me, little English mouse? You think I will take advantage of you? Or perhaps it is yourself you are frightened of, eh? Maybe that is it?'

He was absolutely on the ball there but Sophy would rather have walked on red-hot coals in her bare feet than admit it. 'I am here to keep Jill company,' she said stiffly, 'as you well know. Not to go gadding off with every Tom, Dick or Harry.'

'Forgetting this Tom, Dick and Harry for a moment, you are saying you will not accompany me to dinner tomorrow night because of your responsibility towards Jill?' he said softly. 'That is it?' His expression told her all too clearly what he thought of that.

She glared at him but was saved the embarrassment of a reply by the other three emerging from the open doors of the dining room, Evangelos carrying another carafe of the milky white ouzo in one hand which he raised to Andreas, saying, 'It is a night for sitting and drinking while we put the world to rights, yes?'

'Sorry, but no.' Andreas rose lazily to his feet, his smiling face taking in the others as he said, 'I've some papers to look at tonight at home and Paul has been waiting outside for the last few minutes. I told him we were leaving at ten-thirty.'

'All work and no play?' Dimitra was smiling at her son

as she spoke and it was clear the bond between them was a strong one.

'That has never been one of my attributes—or failings, depending on which way you look at it,' Andreas returned drily. 'But it might apply more aptly to Sophy. Do you know she is insisting she cannot be my guest at the Pallini tomorrow because she is here only as Jill's companion?'

The dirty, rotten rat. Sophy was too taken aback by the effortless fait accompli to say anything as the others instantly voiced their insistence that of *course* she must go out for the night and enjoy herself. They wouldn't hear otherwise.

'You don't need to keep me company, Sophy, you know that,' Jill said earnestly.

Her voice had barely finished before Dimitra was saying, 'Please, Sophy, I hope we have not made you feel you are only here in some minor capacity. We love having you stay with us, my dear, but you are perfectly free to come and go as you wish, and I promise you we will take good care of Jill.'

Only Evangelos remained silent, his dark eyes on his son's face as Andreas smiled easily, saying, 'You see, Sophy? This is your holiday too, and you will be doing me a great honour in allowing me to show you a little of the real Greece while you are here, starting tomorrow night, yes?'

He had backed her into a corner and there was absolutely no way out without making it clear they were at loggerheads, and thereby upsetting everyone and causing tension. If ever there was a sly, underhand double-dealer, Andreas Karydis was one, Sophy thought furiously as she fought not to betray her thoughts.

And further proof of this came when Andreas turned to Jill, his voice pleasant as he said, 'Of course you are more than welcome to come too, Jill, although I thought you would prefer to remain close to the house in case Michael should wake up and want you.'

'Definitely,' Jill agreed at once.

As he had known she would. Sophy bent down and fiddled with the strap of her sandal, pretending it was undone, in an effort to hide the contortions her face had fallen into as she struggled not to scream abuse at him. Who did he think he was, manipulating everyone like this? Talk about a cheek! He thought he was so clever. It was a good thirty seconds before she could trust both her face and her voice, and even then her voice had a clipped edge to it when she said, 'What time would you like me to be ready?'

'Seven okay?' he returned easily, the charm fairly oozing out of him. 'And it's smart casual, not dinner dress, at the Pallini, unless you would like to go somewhere more formal?'

'The Pallini will be fine,' Sophy answered hollowly, wondering what the reaction would be if she threw the last of her cool coffee into his face.

'Until seven tomorrow, then.' He smiled at her, nodded at the others and kissed his mother lightly on the forehead before walking into the house, leaving Sophy sitting in a state of semi-shock as she listened to the others talking. She heard his voice once he was outside the house again—obviously conversing with Paul—and then the sound of a car's engine and the scrunch of tyres as it drew away.

Well, okay, Andreas Karydis, she thought furiously, I might be having dinner with you tomorrow night but that will be all. If you think for one second you can twist me round your little finger like you seem to do everyone else, you've got a big shock coming. She frowned to herself and then something made her glance up to see Evangelos watching her, his eyes—Andreas's eyes—narrowed and thoughtful.

She forced a smile and made a light, complimentary remark about the beautiful gardens, and Evangelos immediately switched into attentive host mode, the awkward moment passing.

But an hour or so later, when the four of them rose to retire, Evangelos caught her arm as they walked into the house letting Dimitra and Jill walk on ahead of them. 'He has annoyed you,' Evangelos said quietly, the words a statement and not a question. And he didn't need to mention Andreas's name.

Sophy thought about prevaricating but somehow, with Evangelos's kind eyes fixed on her face, it wasn't an honest option. 'Yes,' she said simply as they stood in the middle of the dining room looking at each other. 'He has.'

'You do not want to go to dinner with Andreas?' There was no condemnation in the question, merely mild and somewhat surprised enquiry. 'I think you will enjoy yourself at the Pallini.'

Did she want to be with him? The idea was thrilling on the one hand, but possessed of such danger she couldn't ignore the tension the thought produced. Also, the way he had manipulated her had caught her on the raw, to the point where she would have given anything to throw his dinner back in his face! And all these feelings, every one of them, was so alien to the calm, composed and matter-of-fact woman she normally was that she felt she didn't know herself anymore. So all in all, no—she didn't think she wanted to go to dinner with Evangelos's son!

Sophy was aware as she looked into the handsome face of Andreas's father that she was seeing Andreas as he would be in thirty years or so, and it took a moment for her to say quietly, 'I prefer to make my own mind up on such matters,' and this time she knew she *had* avoided a direct answer.

'I can understand this. Andreas can be...persistent when

his mind is set on something.' Evangelos's voice was apologetic.

Persistent? Persistent didn't even *begin* to describe it!

Sophy's face must have given her away because in the next instant Evangelos chuckled quietly, and his voice carried the amusement evident in his face when he said, 'It would be good for Andreas to find he cannot have things all his own way for once. He is used—' He stopped abruptly and then said, 'Pardon me, Sophy. May I speak frankly?' And at her nod, continued, 'My son is used to being the pursued rather than the pursuer, you know what I mean? He is wealthy and good-looking, and this has a magnetism all of its own for some women. Most women.'

Sophy stared at Evangelos, not at all sure if Andreas's father was warning her off his son or quite the reverse. 'This is not good for someone of Andreas's disposition,' Evangelos continued after a moment or two, 'because it produces a feeling of contempt in him for the women concerned. He is a highly intelligent man and tires easily of being told what he knows the woman concerned imagines he wishes to hear.'

Sophy nodded. Yes, she could understand that. Wealth and privilege brought its own problems. Her brow wrinkled. 'I don't quite see why you are telling me all this,' she said quietly. 'I have absolutely no intention of flattering Andreas's ego.' Not if he was the last man on earth!

'I know that, my dear.' Evangelos patted her arm in a fatherly fashion. 'I am merely explaining the reason for my son's lack of…sensitivity this evening.'

'Right.' She didn't quite understand where this was going.

'But one thing I would add, Sophy.' As she went to walk on Evangelos stopped her for a moment more. 'Andreas has had his fair share of hurt and disappointment, some of which—when combined with what I have already said—

has produced a cynicism which it has grieved me to see. He is a good man, a very good man but a complicated one.'

This whole family was complicated. Complicated enough to make her wish she had never suggested accompanying Jill out here. Sophy stitched a smile on her face with some effort and said quietly, 'I suppose we all are underneath the façade we put on for the rest of the world. My mother used to say—' She paused, not sure if she wanted to continue what she had started to say. This was Andreas's father, after all.

'Yes?' Evangelos asked mildly. 'What did your mother say?'

Sophy dismissed the feeling that she was letting Andreas's father persuade her to reveal too much. 'She used to say that men and women could only be their true selves with very young children and babies, or their pets. Never each other. With other adults there was always self-protection built in which formed its own natural barrier.'

'Do you believe that?' Evangelos asked quietly, his eyes intent on her heart shaped face.

Sophy shrugged uncomfortably. 'I'm not sure,' she said carefully. 'My father let my mother down very badly, so certainly after he had left us that was the case for her. Therefore it must be true for a percentage of people.'

'That is very sad.' Andreas's father shook his head slowly. 'For myself, I can say that I am totally myself with Dimitra, and, I believe, she with me. She knows everything there is to know about me—the good, the bad and the ugly.' He smiled at her, his last words aiming to lighten what had suddenly become a very heavy conversation, and Sophy smiled back.

'You're lucky,' she said simply.

'Sometimes we have to go out and secure our luck,' Evangelos murmured quietly. 'This is an age of instant gratification. Instant meals, instant money, instant relationships. But a relationship worth having doesn't happen without constant work and effort, not even the best of them.'

She stared at him, and then as he took her arm and walked her out into the hall where the others were waiting the moment passed.

But later, lying in the warm darkness of her bed, Sophy found she was more confused and disturbed than ever. Everything was wrong somehow and nothing was right, and yet she couldn't really put her finger on what was bothering her so acutely. She frowned irritably in the blackness, turned over with a little sigh and determinedly shut her eyes.

CHAPTER SIX

Sophy didn't sleep at all well. She couldn't remember anything of the dark dreams that had troubled her during the night, but only that they had been of a nature to make her feel disturbed and distressed when she awoke early the next morning.

She showered and dressed, and acted as though she hadn't a care in the world during breakfast with Jill and Michael and Andreas's parents. After exploring the grounds with Michael and playing a couple of games of tennis with him, she and her small nephew spent the rest of the morning in the pool while Jill and Dimitra were taken shopping by Evangelos. Sophy and Michael were included in the invitation by Andreas's parents, but the look on Michael's face at the prospect of a morning spent in shops was enough to induce Sophy to offer to stay at the villa with him.

The others were staying out for lunch, so Christina organised a small simple barbecue by the pool for Sophy and Michael which was great fun, Michael's enthusiasm infecting Sophy.

Once they had eaten, Sophy insisted Michael wasn't allowed in the water for at least an hour and persuaded her nephew to curl up on one of the cushioned sun-loungers for a nap, a beach towel wrapped round him and the shade of a large tree making the temperature comfortable in spite of the baking heat.

Gradually through the morning, Sophy's face had become calm and relaxed in the young child's uncomplicated company, and as she sat sipping at a delicious glass of iced lemonade and watching him sleep, she felt peaceful for the first time since she had set foot in Greece.

She was purposely concentrating on nothing more controversial than the sleeping child, the bright sunshine and scented air, and the lone drone of tiny busy insects in the surrounding vegetation.

She must have drifted off to sleep herself because when the others returned they awoke both her and Michael, and they all spent a happy hour or two chatting over more iced drinks and watching Michael playing in the pool with the enormous plastic cheeky-faced whale Dimitra and Evangelos had bought their grandson.

It was a pleasant time, easy and unhurried, and when—at just gone half-past five—they all returned to the house, Michael to have his tea with Christina and the adults retiring to their rooms to rest before getting ready for dinner, Sophy found herself humming a little tune as she entered her sunlit bedroom. She'd just been overtired before, she told herself firmly.

She had just walked through to the bathroom to run herself a bath, fancying a long luxurious soak rather than a quick shower, when Ainka knocked at her door informing her there was a telephone call for Mrs Fearn and please could she come right away?

'For me?' Sophy asked in surprise, her mind immediately expecting Annie to be on the other end of the wire with some catastrophe necessitating her immediate return to England. She ignored the faint sense of panic and disappointment the thought conjured up and walked across to the bedroom extension, lifting the receiver and speaking her name clearly and crisply.

'Hallo, Sophy.'

The dark smoky voice could only belong to one man on earth, and for a moment the blood rushed in her ears like an express train. She licked suddenly dry lips and said steadily, 'Andreas?' as though she wasn't quite sure. No need to inflate the super ego any more than it was already.

'I am just calling to make sure that seven is still okay?' he said smoothly. 'I understand you have been taking care of Michael today, so if you would prefer to leave a little later after a siesta?'

'No, seven's fine.' She took a deep breath and hoped the gallop of her heart hadn't sounded in her voice. How come all the good the relaxing day had done her had vanished in a moment?

'Great. I'll see you a little later, then.'

She stood with the receiver in her hand for some seconds after the call had finished, until the sound of water reminded her about the bath and sent her hurrying into the en-suite. Suddenly the evening was there in front of her with all its capacity for potential disaster staring her in the face, and as she stripped off her swimming costume and shirt top her mind was buzzing. She should have said she was too tired, ill, anything.

She must not panic, she told herself silently. She would keep him at a distance with cool, reasonable politeness tonight; let him see he couldn't touch her emotions and that the physical chemistry between them was simply mind over matter. Which it was. Of course it was. Otherwise they were no better than animals.

By ten to seven she had changed three times. She'd felt the first dress was too revealing and come-hitherish, the second outfit of a cream linen summer suit too austere, and the third dress in bright bubblegum pink had wiped all the colour out of her skin. Now she surveyed herself in the mirror, her face tragic and her equilibrium completely blown.

The chocolate sequinned top with its spider-web thin straps dressed down beautifully with black jeans and strappy, high-heeled sandals, and she had fixed her hair into a loose casual knot, allowing a few tendrils to wisp about her cheeks and neck. She was wearing just a touch of shadow and mascara but that was all; the sun have given her skin a honey glow no cosmetics could improve and she only ever wore lip-gloss on her lips.

Would he think she had tried too hard? Or maybe that her outfit wasn't dressy enough, or even too dressy? These females who chased him—how would they dress? Designer labels to a woman, no doubt, with real 24-carat little rocks glittering on their necks and throats. She bit her lip hard at the way her thoughts were going and closed her eyes for a moment. Enough. Enough, Sophy Fearn. You don't have to compete with anyone—especially not where Andreas Karydis is concerned, for goodness' sake! Pull yourself together, girl.

She opened her eyes and decided on no jewellery at all except a pair of simple silver studs in her ears. Ready or not, here I come... The simple childish rhyme she and Jill had used so often in their games of hide-and-seek when they were young made her smile for a second. There was no doubt Andreas Karydis would be ready and perfectly in control, but she herself was quite a different matter.

She remembered again his compelling sexuality and the effortless ease with which he had kissed her and smashed through all her defences, and her heart began to pound madly. When Jill knocked the door the next moment and popped her head round to say Andreas had just arrived, it was almost a relief to know the moment was here and the waiting was over.

'You look gorgeous, Sophy, just right,' Jill said approvingly.

Evangelos had told the girls that the Pallini was a favourite with the younger generation, an excellent restaurant with its own dance floor and band but with an informal reputation that meant almost anything went in the clothes line.

'Are you sure?' Sophy asked anxiously. 'What's Andreas wearing? He hasn't dressed up, has he?'

'I don't think so.' Observant had never been a word which could be applied to Jill. 'Smart casual, like you.'

Smart casual could possibly have described the midnight blue silk shirt and beautifully cut black designer trousers that sat on Andreas's frame like an advertisement for sensuality, but sheer dynamite would have been more apt, Sophy thought weakly as she walked into the drawing room some moments later.

'Good evening, Sophy.' Andreas moved from his position at Evangelos's side to stand looking down at her, his grey eyes frankly appreciative. 'You look very lovely tonight.'

'Thank you.' She tried to match his smoothness but felt the warmth in her cheeks and knew she was blushing.

'All ready?' He turned as he spoke and raised a casual hand of farewell to the others who were all trying—unsuccessfully in the most part—to hide their interest in the proceedings.

Sophy was vitally aware of Andreas as they walked out to the car, and after smiling at the impassive Paul sitting in the front seat she climbed into the back of the sleek limousine, catching a whiff of expensive aftershave as Andreas climbed in beside her.

'Pallini's isn't far.' Andreas settled himself comfortably beside her, apparently unaware that he brushed her body once or twice in the process with a hard male thigh. She, on the other hand, felt the contact like electric shocks and had to apply rigid control not to let it show.

The whole point of the evening was to let this impossible man know she was quite oblivious to him, not behave like a cat on a hot tin roof, she told herself desperately.

She expected him to turn on the charm big time but, after the few brief words when they had entered the car, Andreas was quite silent as they left the estate and turned on to the narrow lane outside. They had reached the main road and been travelling for some minutes before he said quietly, 'Are you hungry?'

'So, so.' It was a beautiful evening, the sky still cornflower-blue and mellow sunlight slanting in the car window. 'Michael and I had a barbecue together at lunchtime and I made the mistake of eating the food he didn't want as well as my own,' she said a touch ruefully, 'so I'm not ravenous, if that's what you are asking.'

'Good.' He smiled at her, an easy smile that smoothed out the hard angles and planes of his face. 'I've reserved a table for nine; I thought it might be nice to take a stroll along the beach first. It is always beautiful in the evening, I think.'

'Fine,' she said with a wariness she couldn't quite hide, and then found herself stiffening as he leant across and took her hand in his. She stared into his eyes, her own wide.

'I am going to hold your hand, Sophy,' he said with the ghost of a smile twisting his lips. 'Okay? That gets that one out into the open. I shall probably hold it on the beach as well and put my arm round you, along with other little gestures that come naturally when a man is with a woman. I am not going to regress to the agony of adolescence with all its fumblings and awkwardness, so can you relax and accept you are out on a date?'

'A date?' She stared at him, horrified. And Andreas Karydis, even as an adolescent, would never, *ever* have fumbled, awkwardly or otherwise, her mind stated silently. 'This isn't a date. You're Theodore's brother,' she said a little stupidly.

'His half-brother,' he reminded her evenly, 'and as far as I know the one doesn't preclude the other. This *is* a date,

Sophy, whether you like it or not, and if you give yourself half a chance you might find you actually enjoy it.'

'Enjoy being with you, you mean,' she said before she actually thought what she was saying.

He smiled, apparently not in the least put out. 'Exactly,' he said drily, 'and don't expect me to apologise for suggesting such an outrageous notion, either. Woman is expected to be man's companion. It is the right and proper order of things.'

He was teasing her and she knew it, and she smiled weakly.

The long sandy beaches and clear turquoise water in the north of Greece were renowned for their charm, but the exquisite, gently shelving stretch on which the Pallini was situated was particularly lovely, being just off the normal tourist track.

They had just passed through a small town which had been a winding maze of narrow cobbled streets and tiny squares, with flower-bedecked tavernas and sugar white houses spilling out on to the pavements. Just outside the perimeters of the town, Paul had turned the car off the main road on to a well-used track, which had opened immediately to disclose a large sprawling one-storey building built of wood, with an enormous veranda stretching the length of it which was painted white.

Massive wooden barrels stood to one side of the building, and the front of it was decorated with fishermen's nets, huge shells, pieces of driftwood and other objects the sea had obviously brought to its door in its time. The effect was very attractive.

People were already sitting eating on the veranda as well as inside the massive restaurant, and other couples were idly enjoying a drink in the evening sunshine on the many scattered tables and chairs on the beach in front and to the sides of the building. Music drifted out on to the warm air along with the sound of conversation and laughter, and there was a definite buzz in the air.

In the distance across the white glistening sand, tiny waves lapped gently against the shoreline, the odd bird or two—along with two-legged creatures of the human variety—wandering along the beach in the warmth of the dying day. It was so foreign, so easy and relaxed and utterly Greek, that for a moment Sophy just stood and drank it all in once they were out of the car and Paul had disappeared. Sun, sea, sand…and Andreas at her side.

'What an unusual place,' she said at last, conscious of Andreas's eyes on her face in the moments before she turned and looked at him. 'And it seems to be very popular.'

He nodded, his dark eyes narrowed against the sunlight as he took her hand and began walking towards the building. 'A good friend of mine owns it,' he said quietly, and then, as Sophy bent and slipped her feet out of her sandals, he waited until she had straightened again before taking her hand and continuing, 'Nick's family is a wealthy one but he is the original bohemian. I think his father was despairing that he'd ever do anything with his life and then Nick met Iona, and within three months he had married her and bought this beach front, all of it. They built the restaurant and it was a success from day one. That was ten years ago.'

She couldn't resist saying, 'The love of a good woman obviously worked wonders then?' as she smiled mockingly.

'Obviously.' It was very dry.

'Is there living accommodation at the back?' she asked curiously as they approached the rambling building.

'Uh-huh. Just a kitchen and bathroom and one bedroom and sitting room. They live here eight months of the year and just retire to their house—a beauty of a place—for the winter.'

Sophy cast her eyes again over the wide sweep of sand

and sea lit by strong evening Greek sunlight. 'An idyllic lifestyle.'

'In many respects. The restaurant only opens in the evenings as they didn't want to lose sight of having time together, and they have an army of chefs and waiters now. However, money cannot buy everything.'

She raised her eyebrows questioningly at the statement, spoken as it was in an unusually sober tone for Andreas.

'Iona cannot have a child of her own,' he said quietly. They had reached the foot of the stairs leading up to the veranda now, and his voice changed as he said, 'Come and meet Nick and Iona and then we will walk a little of your lunch off, yes? Then you will have room for more.'

There was no time to reply before a little squeal from within the restaurant reached them, and in the next moment a small, slender woman with long brown hair reaching to her waist had flung herself down the steps and into Andreas's arms. 'Andreas! Oh, it's so good to see you! But you are very, very naughty. It has been months since you came to see us.'

'Don't exaggerate, Iona.' A long, loose-limbed and floppy-haired man had followed his wife and now he smiled at Sophy, holding out his hand as he said, 'You must be Sophy. I'm Nick and this limpet clinging to Andreas is my wife, Iona.'

During the next few minutes Sophy decided she liked Andreas's friends and that, if the circumstances had been different, they were the sort of people she would have liked to get to know better and spend time with.

Nick was the antithesis of Andreas, being so laid-back and mild-tempered that it was impossible to imagine him ever getting upset about anything, and Iona was just a sweetheart. Tiny, with huge expressive brown eyes and a gentleness about her that was very pleasant, she clearly adored her handsome husband, and he her. It was very nice to see, Sophy decided.

'Give me a bottle of wine and two glasses, Nick,' Andreas said after a while. 'We're going for a walk on the beach but we'll be back for nine. Has Iona made any of her famous tzatziki, by any chance? And it has to be Iona's, not one of your chefs, good as they are,' he added with a wink at his friend.

'Don't I always make some if I know you're coming?' Iona answered reproachfully.

'Always,' Andreas agreed easily, smiling as he bent and kissed Iona's smooth forehead. 'And it's always perfect.'

Sophy could hear Nick shouting orders in Greek to someone, and then he was back with a bottle of dark red wine and two enormous wine glasses which he passed to Andreas, saying as he did so, 'I've told Stephanos to save a couple of good portions of moussaka along with a bowl of extra prawns and shrimps. I presume you'll want your favourite main course after the tzatziki?'

'I've been tasting it all day.' Andreas grinned back.

Sophy was feeling acutely disturbed as they left the busy bustle of the restaurant and walked down the steps of the veranda on to the smooth white sand. She had left her sandals in Iona's care, and now, as she curled her toes into the warm powdery grains beneath her feet, she said quietly, 'They're lovely people. I presume they spoke English for my benefit?'

'They would want to make you feel welcome,' Andreas agreed softly. 'And, yes, they are two of the best.'

She didn't like what seeing him relaxed and off guard with his friends had done to her equilibrium. He had been different with Nick and Iona to how he had appeared before, even with his family. Younger, softer, more approachable. And infinitely more dangerous because this Andreas was more attractive than ever.

There were tiny shells here and there, shining and glistening as they made their way right up to the water's edge until the low hum of noise from the restaurant behind them was gone. Andreas had taken her hand in his as they had walked, the bottle of wine and the stems of the wine glasses hanging loosely in his other hand, and for some ten minutes or so he didn't break the silence which had fallen between them.

Sophy was breathing in the scent of the sea and sand and warm summer air, looking across the miles of calm tranquil turquoise water under the vivid, hard blue Greek sky as she concentrated on not thinking at all. If she started to think she was quite liable to panic, she'd admitted to herself at the beginning of their stroll, and so it was easier to blank her mind and let her senses soak up the beautiful evening. Ignoring the hard-muscled figure at the side of her was more difficult because her body seemed to have developed a life of its own since she had met Andreas.

'Over there.' Their area of beach was quite deserted now and Andreas was pointing to where a shelf of rock curved gently out of the sand, the water rippling daintily round its edges. 'The perfect place to sit and have a glass of wine and tell each other our life stories,' he drawled lazily.

She glanced at him quickly. 'I don't remember that that was part of the deal tonight.'

His grin flashed without apology. 'What would you like to talk about, then?' he asked very softly. 'The choice is yours.'

She decided to treat this lightly and gave him a noncommital smile she was rather proud of in the circumstances. 'Tell me about Greece,' she suggested evenly as they reached the smooth polished surface of the warm rock and perched comfortably, looking out over the glassy, still water.

Andreas gave her an amused glance from dark cynical

eyes as he poured two glasses of the rich blackcurrant wine and then handed her hers. 'You can get a guide book for that.'

The sun was sinking lower, flirting with the prospect of letting the moon have pre-eminence, and Sophy took several sips of the wine—which was perfectly wonderful—before she said, 'Okay, tell me about your work, then. Detail your average day. All men like to talk about their jobs, don't they?'

'When they are in the company of a beautiful woman?' Andreas said with a distaste that was not totally feigned. 'I think you have been associating with the wrong sort of man, Sophy.'

'You are being deliberately difficult.'

'Not at all.' He let his eyes sweep over her lovely face and something in his gaze brought the colour surging into her cheeks. 'Tell me about him, your husband,' Andreas said very quietly, all amusement gone from his dark face. 'Were you happy? Was he good to you?'

It was totally unexpected and for a moment all she could do was to stare at him, her eyes wide. And then she took a deep breath and said just as quietly, 'Yes, we were happy. Matthew was a good man and I loved him.'

The dark face didn't change by so much as the flicker of an eyelash. 'Is it painful to talk about him?'

'Painful?' She turned her profile to him, looking out to sea again. 'Not now,' she said slowly. The memories she had of Matthew were precious and warm, but they were in the past. She had moved on. 'But he didn't deserve to die so young.'

'Tell me what happened,' Andreas said quietly. 'I want to know.'

So she told him it all, from when she and Matthew had first met at university until the night he had died in her arms. 'I couldn't believe it at first,' she said quietly. 'He was my best friend and then suddenly he wasn't there any more.'

Andreas had said nothing whilst she had talked, but now he refilled her glass before saying softly, 'Did you mourn him as a friend or a husband, Sophy?'

'What?' She was too shocked to say anything more.

'I am sure you loved him, but fire can never be wholly content with water.'

'I don't know what you are talking about.' She glared at him angrily, not sure if he was criticising her or Matthew or whether any criticism was intended at all.

'Water is calm and tranquil, undisturbed by the more turbulent emotions that drive some men and women,' Andreas said softly. 'Some of the greatest statesmen in the world have had such attributes, but you...you were not meant to be the wife of such. Fire must be met with fire or else it slowly becomes quenched and reduced to the merest flicker. Fire is passion and wildness. It is fierce and frantic and life itself.'

Her chin was up, but something in the intensity of his voice caused her not to be as angry as she felt she should be. But he was all but telling her she shouldn't have married Matthew, wasn't he? Or at least that they would have proved to be unhappy in time—and all this when she'd only known him a couple of days. How dared he say whether they had been right for each other or not? But...somehow he wasn't being nasty.

'You didn't know Matthew,' she said coolly, 'and frankly you don't know me either, so I fail to see how you can say anything about our marriage.'

'I have heard and seen how you talked about him tonight.' His eyes had locked on hers and the rosy light that was now bathing the sky in the first signs of dusk made his bronzed skin and black hair even darker.

Sophy stared at him a moment longer and then slid off

the rock on to her feet. He couldn't be allowed to affect her so deeply. She took a gulp of the wine and then, as Andreas reached for the glass in her hand and took it from her, became still. He placed it beside his own glass on the smooth stone and then turned her into him, his hands about her waist.

'You are angry with me,' he murmured softly, but without any regret in his voice that she could hear.

'Why would I be angry?' she said icily, wishing she had the power to send him tumbling away from her if she pushed him, but knowing she wouldn't make any impression at all on the hard, muscled chest. 'You tell me I shouldn't have married my husband and that we were unsuited, when you never even met Matthew! How could I possibly object to that? Of course, some people might call it arrogant in the extreme, but no doubt that wouldn't bother you for a second. It wouldn't, would it?'

'Do you want a lie to smooth your ruffled feathers or the truth?' he asked mildly.

She opened her mouth to tell him exactly what he could do with his amateur psychology when his mouth closed over hers, hot and stunningly sweet as his hands moved her firmly into his body. It was a smooth and experienced move and allowed no opportunity for escape, not that Sophy was thinking of it anyway.

He explored her mouth leisurely but with an exquisite finesse that spoke volumes about his knowledge of women, and the scent of the sea and sand combined with the overwhelming enchantment that was taking her over.

Somehow her arms had wound round his neck, although she hadn't been aware of it, only that the smell and feel of him was all about her and she didn't want it to stop.

His hands were in the silk of her hair, turning her head to gain even greater access to her mouth before his lips began to cover her face and throat and ears in hot little burning kisses that made her moan low in her throat. And then the devastatingly knowing mouth was nibbling at her lips again, provoking a response that Sophy could no more have denied than she could have stopped breathing.

Andreas was breathing hard, his chest rising and falling under the thin silk of his shirt, but his control was absolute, and after a few last lingering kisses he moved her gently from him, looking down into her dazed eyes with an un-fathomable expression. 'So, we know how we would settle any disputes between us, eh?' he said softly.

Sophy was trying to ignore the tingling in her spine and the slow languorous warmth that had weakened her limbs and sent her dizzy, but his words—with their underlying message of some sort of future involvement—sent a healthy shot of adrenalin into her blood. 'There is and will be no "us",' she said fairly steadily, 'so that's a purely rhetorical question, I take it?'

'You can take it any way you want to,' he answered pleasantly, but with just the faintest touch of steel under-lying the smoothness. 'But for now we will return to the Pallini and eat well. We will smile and converse and speak of nothing more controversial than whether the moussaka is to your taste. You do like moussaka?' he added easily.

'Yes, Andreas, I like moussaka.'

If he noticed the cool flat note of control in her voice he didn't comment, merely gathering up the almost empty bot-tle of wine and the two glasses and following her as she began to walk back down the beach. And this time he did not take her hand. Ridiculously, Sophy felt bereft.

Sophy had not expected to enjoy the rest of the evening but—annoyingly—she found she couldn't help it.

The meal was wonderful but of gargantuan proportions, beginning with Iona's tzatziki, a dish made with yoghurt and garlic and served in two small bowls with warm chunks of fresh garlic bread to scoop it up with. The moussaka was heavenly but she was openly amazed at the amount Andreas put away, and he still found room for a healthy portion of a pastry dessert oozing with honey and cream and succulent red cherries.

They ate on the veranda overlooking the sea, the breeze off the water taking the edge of the humid heat and making it very pleasant. The sun went down in a riveting display of colour, rivers of red and gold and cinnamon flowing across the soft charcoal grey and midnight blue in a stunning extravaganza of nature at her best. It was hypnotic and spell-binding and the stuff dreams were made of.

And so was Andreas. Sophy knew he had set out to charm her, but in spite of herself she couldn't help responding. He was amusing and attentive, telling the odd funny story directed against himself with a wicked self-efface-ment that stated quite clearly he was deliberately being dep-recative to win her round. The dark eyes flashed with hu-mour and in the dim light his face had taken on something of the appearance of a handsome bronze statue, his features purely male and classical and his hair as black as the night.

She was enjoying herself, so much, and she didn't *want* to—but he made it impossible not to. And as though he had picked up on her thoughts, he leant closer to her as they sipped their coffee and brandy, his voice low and smoky as he said quietly, 'You should relax more often, but you find it hard to let go, don't you? If it wasn't your marriage that made you that way, then what? Because, deep, deep inside, I do not think you're like that.'

She stared back at him, suddenly finding the warm scru-tiny unnerving. She opened her mouth to make some airy light comment but instead found herself saying, 'The way we were brought up, I suppose. My mother had to work all the time and Jill... Well, I guess I felt I had to look after her somehow. She always seemed younger than me, much younger, even though we're twins.'

Andreas nodded slowly. 'Your father?'

'Left the bosom of his family when Jill and I were a couple of months old,' she said, not as flatly as she would have liked. It was the wine, she told herself irritably. She had drunk just enough to make the mask slip a little. She had to be careful.

He had picked up the thread of bitterness. 'Your mother didn't marry again?' he asked softly.

''How could she? She worked all the hours under the sun; there was no time for socialising or meeting anyone. Besides, I think she still loved my father, although she would rather have died than admit it. She knew he was a weak, worthless rat but she couldn't quite let go.'

The faint air of bewilderment caused his mouth to tighten for a moment before he said, 'Do you ever see him?'

'I've never seen him.' Sophy straightened in her chair and the body language and the crispness of her voice told him the conversation was over. 'He might be dead, for all I know.' And then she smiled, a brittle smile, as she said, 'Could I have another brandy, please?'

A spirit of recklessness had taken her over and suddenly she didn't want to think any more. He had said she found it hard to relax and let go, and it was true when she thought about it. She had been on the treadmill of life for as long as she could remember, always being responsible and rational and in control. Even with Matthew it had seemed natural to them both that she would make the final decision on things. Not that she had minded, she told herself quickly, as though the thought was a betrayal; in fact, she had liked it being that way...hadn't she?

Suddenly she wasn't sure about anything—and it was a frightening feeling. The urge to chill out, to let her hair down without any thought of the consequences was as strong as it was dangerous, and she had to master it now, right this minute.

She felt obliged to drink the second glass of brandy when it came but washed it down with two cups of strong black coffee, the fleeting moments of devil-may-care foolhardiness vanishing almost as soon as they had arrived. But they were a warning, she told herself soberly, as she watched Andreas's face as he talked to Iona and Nick who had joined them at their table.

Andreas was a complex, enigmatic man and she didn't have a clue what made him tick. That kiss had told her he was as far out of her league, sexually and in every other way, as the man in the moon. And he was a man who liked women, and they liked him back.

Behind them in the distance where the beach road ran came the low whisper of cypress trees teased by the soft warm breeze, and the night sky was bright with stars, the moon sailing resplendent and proud surrounded by her lesser subjects. There were fewer people left now but the band was still playing, and the dance floor was not as crowded as it had been whilst they had eaten, just the odd couple dancing dreamily to a slow ballad.

'Come.' Andreas stood to his feet, extending his hand towards her. 'We will dance a little.'

'Oh, no,' she said immediately. 'I'm not a good dancer.'

She might as well have saved her breath because she found herself lifted to her feet with an authoritative hand and whisked through to the interior of the building, Iona and Nick following in their wake. She nerved herself for the moment when he took her into his arms and consequently was as stiff as a board, earning a little click of annoyance from Andreas. 'Relax, let the music lead you,' he murmured softly in her ear, his male warmth enclosing her in its own magic. 'It is not a sin to be young and carefree.'

Carefree, no. Careless, yes. And the two were dangerously entwined tonight.

'Is there anyone special in England?' he asked her quietly after they had danced for a minute or two.

'Not really,' she answered, trying to make it sound as though she had a whole regiment of boyfriends to choose from. 'Any relationships have to fit in with my work schedule, which can be hectic at times.' Or they would if she had any relationships!

'And your friends—your men friends—are content with this?' Andreas asked disapprovingly. 'Did Matthew fit in with your work schedule, too?'

'That's really none of your business.' It was hard to sound as vinegary as she would have liked when she was being held against his hard muscled frame, and his breath was ruffling her hair. But it was such a typical Andreas comment!

'Of course it isn't,' he agreed immediately. 'So, did he?'

Sophy's head shot up, her violet-blue eyes expressing her indignation. 'You really don't take no for an answer, do you?' she said tartly. 'I've never met anyone so confrontational.'

He smiled, tightening his arms. 'How clever of you to notice. So, the men in your life have always come to heel, yes?'

'I refuse to discuss this with you.' It was angry and hissed through gritted teeth, and suddenly—to Sophy's astonishment—Andreas threw back his head on a roar of laughter.

'Defiant to the last,' he murmured when he'd finished laughing. 'What is this myth about English women being so cucumber-cool, eh? You are more fiery than any Greek girl I know.'

Sophy gave him a dry look that made him grin again. 'Is that supposed to be some kind of compliment?' she said with a primness that made his smile widen. 'Greek style?'

'You don't like compliments?' he murmured silkily.

'Not when they can't be trusted.'

'What a suspicious little cat you are, my sweet.' He fitted her into him again and Sophy gave up trying to argue. She would never win in a war of words with Andreas; he was a man with all the answers. Which was another reason to keep him at arm's length.

Nevertheless she couldn't deny that she felt more alive than she'd felt for a long time, perhaps ever. But that wasn't just Andreas, she tried to reassure herself silently. It was the holiday magic of foreign parts; the warmth, the atmosphere, the sheer exoticness of it all. It got into your blood.

Sophy had expected they would leave shortly after they finished eating, but as the time continued to roll by she found the large group of people who were left were what Iona and Nick called their regulars—friends and patrons who regularly stayed until the early hours. And she didn't want to leave, not really. She was having too good a time.

The wine and ouzo was flowing freely and there was an earthier flavour to the mood inside the restaurant now. Iona and Nick sat with them at a table close to the dance floor when the four of them weren't dancing, and they were wonderful company. Nick was funny and Iona was droll and Sophy had never laughed so much in her life. She felt as if she'd known them for ever.

At one point all the men in the place linked arms and began a line of Greek dancing as the music got wilder and wilder, the women clapping and calling as the men stamped and whirled.

Sophy's eyes were fixed on Andreas. He was so different from how he appeared normally. Usually the aura of hard authority and command sat on him like cold armour, radiating ruthlessness along with the virile force that was at the essence of him. But like this, with his friends, he seemed open and relaxed, the cutting edges of his arrogance smoothed to silky softness.

But he was the same man, she reminded herself quickly, wrenching her gaze away from the dark, laughing figure and sipping somewhat frantically at the soft drink she had asked for earlier. He had a life force that was pure vital dangerous energy, an intensity of spirit that would always subdue and subjugate those around him.

Her fingers tightened on the glass and her heart began to thud. Why was she here? Why hadn't she made some excuse at the last minute? A headache or something along those lines?'

Because she had been curious. The answer was very clear in her head and suddenly there was no trace of the faint muzziness the wine had caused earlier. He fascinated her, like some dark alien being from another world, and she had wanted to be with him, wanted to learn more about him. It was almost a relief to acknowledge her weakness now she had let it out of her subconscious.

She had thought the more she learnt, the more she would be able to control this strange feeling she had for him; that in some way he would... What, exactly? Put her off him? Say or do something crass or gross? Maybe she had just *hoped* that would happen without really believing it.

The thoughts were terribly disturbing, and as a roar of laughter and shouting from the men finished the dance to the calls and claps from the women, she forced herself to come out of the deep void she'd sunk into. She would think of all this tomorrow, not now. For now she just had to be on her guard and sensible.

Sensible, level-headed Sophy. All her life these attributes had been tattooed across her forehead, put there by those who knew her best. 'Sophy will see to it.' How often had she heard her mother say that from when she was a tiny child? 'Sophy is my right-hand man.' And she hadn't minded, oh, she hadn't. Her poor mother had had enough to cope with; but now, when she thought about it, the pressure had always been there to take charge and supervise. To behave far older than her years.

'Bossy' had always been written on her school reports somewhere or other, along with 'Sophy has a mind of her own'. But those teachers hadn't known she had gone home to organise tea for herself and Jill from the age of five or six, often doing what housework she could and making it into a game for Jill who was disinclined to work unless she had to.

Oh, what was she doing, thinking all this now? She had never had thoughts like this before, so why now, in the most inappropriate of places? It must be the wine and the rich food.

'What's the matter?' She hadn't been aware Andreas had returned so quickly, but now he bent down and tilted her chin with his finger, his eyes serious. 'What's happened?'

'Nothing has happened.' She forced herself not to react badly.

'You've gone into Spartan mode again,' he said with quiet flatness. 'I can see it in your eyes. For a little while you forgot you mustn't enjoy yourself, didn't you?'

'Don't be ridiculous,' she said too emphatically. 'I often enjoy myself.'

'No, you don't, not really.' He bent closer and kissed her lightly on the lips. 'But you will if I have anything to do with it. Oh, yes, you will. And that is a promise, Sophy.'

And then he turned and spoke to Nick, leaving her sitting in stunned silence at the quiet intensity with which he had murmured the last words.

Why should she be keeping herself in a constant state of frayed nerves over this man? she asked herself silently. She hadn't known a moment's peace since she had first set eyes on him, not really. And she could hardly believe she hadn't known of his existence until a few days ago. She had to get this whole affair into perspective, and once she had done that... She bit down on her lip hard. Then she would know some peace again.

CHAPTER SEVEN

WHEN Sophy awoke to the sunlight streaming in to her room through the balcony windows she had left open the night before, she was surprised she had slept so well.

She and Andreas hadn't left the Pallini until gone three in the morning, and when they had walked along the beach to where Paul was waiting with the car, she had been convinced Andreas would try to make love to her on the way home. But he hadn't so much as kissed her, not until they had reached his parents' front door that was, and even then it had been the sort of social peck that didn't mean anything. Polite, brief and dismissive.

He had returned to the car immediately he had opened the door for her, sliding into the front with Paul this time and raising a laconic hand in farewell as the big car had executed an about turn and whisked off down the drive.

Perversely, his lack of ardour had thoroughly upset her, and she had marched up the stairs to her room, reiterating over and over again that she wanted *nothing* to do with Andreas Karydis and that she was glad—very, *very* glad— that he'd had the good sense at long last to realise that and admit defeat in the seduction stakes. Which that goodnight peck clearly said he had.

She had showered and washed her hair, swiftly blow-drying it before climbing into bed and pulling the thin cotton covers up to her chin as her mind had continued to dissect the evening frame by frame. After telling herself that she would be awake all night, she must have fallen immediately asleep!

She glanced at the little alarm clock she had brought with

her from England and was horrified to see it was eleven o'clock. *Eleven o'clock!* She flung back the covers and leapt out of bed. What must Dimitra and Evangelos be thinking? This was the second time she had missed breakfast and she'd only been here three days!

After a hasty wash in the en-suite bathroom, she threw on a light blue cotton top and matching shorts, and after brushing her hair into sleek obedience ran quickly downstairs without bothering with any make-up. She met Ainka leaving the drawing room with a duster in her hand, and the little maid informed her that the others had gone to visit friends of Dimitra after breakfast, who had a son the same age as Michael. 'Madam thought it would be good for the little one to have someone his own age to play with,' Ainka explained in her soft melodious voice, 'and you were sleeping so soundly, they did not wish to disturb you. Madam left instructions for your breakfast to be served in the sunshine on the patio, yes? I will bring it immediately.'

'Thank you, Ainka.'

So she ate in solitary splendour as she looked out over the beautiful grounds ablaze with sunshine, which was just what she'd needed in truth. It gave her a chance to compose herself and decide what she was going to say before she saw Jill, who, she knew, would want chapter and verse on the previous evening's happenings. She groaned inwardly and tried to marshall her thoughts.

She would be factual, she decided eventually as she finished the last slice of toast heavily covered with cherry preserve and licked sticky fingers appreciatively. Why did food always taste a million times better al fresco? Especially in the sunshine.

Yes, she'd be factual. She'd concentrate on the wonderful restaurant and Andreas's friends and the fact that she had had a lovely time. Their more intimate conversations, the kiss, his comment after the dancing—that she would keep to herself. Because it all meant nothing anyway and she didn't want Jill to get the wrong idea.

She shifted in her seat, suddenly restless. Why hadn't he tried to kiss her in the car, though? And all the way home she had been preparing herself with a mental list of excuses as to why she couldn't go out alone with him again, and then he hadn't even suggested repeating their date, anyway! She felt such a fool. And she couldn't remember ever feeling this way before. With every other man she'd known, either in business or on a personal level, she had always called the tune and had been in control.

She stood up abruptly, cross with herself and the whole wide world. She needed to take a brisk walk in the sunshine and get a grip on herself, she decided firmly. She had never been able to stand women—or men either, if it came to that—who blew hot one minute and cold the next, who were inconsistent and capricious, and here she was behaving like the worst of them. Wretched man! It was all his fault.

By the time the others returned for a late lunch, Sophy's face was calm again and her manner easy and relaxed—at least on the outside. But the outside was all that mattered, she told herself silently whilst patiently giving Jill a minute by minute account of the previous night's proceedings. She would deal with the inside when she was herself again, but privately. And each day that went by meant she was a day nearer to leaving this place—and Andreas. Strangely the thought was not as comforting as she would have liked it to be.

They all lazed the afternoon away by the pool watching Michael and his new little friend, Stevos—whom Dimitra had brought back to play with Michael for a little while—splashing about in the water. It should have been relaxing, Sophy thought wryly. Jill slept at one point, and she found herself watching her sister's lovely face with a mixture of bewilderment and self-annoyance. Why couldn't she be more like Jill? Jill never fought; she had even been able to live all those years with Theodore in a state of relative peace, whereas Sophy knew she would have committed murder in the first five minutes!

What would Andreas be like to live with? The thought was too dangerous to consider and she brushed it away like a troublesome insect, rising in one lithe graceful movement and shedding her shirt top to reveal her bathing costume beneath, which she had changed into after lunch.

She spent a riotous hour in the pool with Michael and Stevos, playing a noisy game of tag followed by an equally noisy game of piggy in the middle. The small boys had their tea together by the pool, and then when Evangelos and Dimitra rose and suggested driving Stevos home, Sophy came indoors to shower and change.

Now she was alone again she wouldn't admit to the flat feeling which had taken her over in the last couple of hours, nor of the secret expectation that Andreas might drop by on his way home from the office as he had done before. Instead she concentrated on her toilet, making as much effort with her appearance as she would have done for a huge dinner party rather than a meal with Jill and her sister's in-laws. Somehow looking good mattered today.

They had just started on the main course when the telephone rang, and the next moment Ainka appeared in the entrance to the dining room, stating Sophy was wanted on the phone. Somewhat mystified as to who would be calling her and assuming it *had* to be Annie with some kind of work problem, this time, she excused herself and walked out into the hall.

'Hello, this is Sophy Fearn,' she said carefully into the receiver, fully expecting Annie's apologetic voice in reply.

'Hello, Sophy Fearn.' The deep smoky voice made her name into a caress and in spite of herself she shivered. 'I was called to Athens today on business and I am stuck here tonight. I assume you're in the middle of dinner, knowing my mother's routine so I won't keep you. I'll pick you up about six tomorrow so be ready, okay? And don't eat too much lunch, this time.'

'What?' She stared into the receiver as her thought process hiccuped and stood still, and then managed to say, 'I don't think so, Andreas. I don't feel it's right to leave Jill like this, besides which it seems very rude as far as your parents are concerned.'

'We've been through that and the consensus of opinion is that it is rubbish.' There was no room for disagreement in the determined, cool voice. 'No one is thinking like that, Sophy.'

Bulldozer approach again. Sophy took a deep breath and said, 'Be that as it may, it's what *I* think.'

'I do not think that is the reason at all. You are frightened to be with me, that is the truth, is it not? Admit it.'

'Now it's you who's talking rubbish,' Sophy lied hotly.

'Prove it. Come out with me tomorrow night,' he said quickly.

'No.' It was a flat refusal and she didn't bother to dress it up with any more excuses. He'd just have to accept no meant no!

'That's settled, then. Six it is.' And the phone went dead.

She couldn't quite believe it. For a moment or two she was so taken aback, she just stared out into the immaculate quiet hall, hearing the low hum of conversation from behind the dining room door and then Jill's laughter and the rumble of Evangelos's distinctive chuckle through the buzzing in her ears. He had hung up on her. *Hung up on her.* And after railroading her into a date she didn't want and had said no to. An emphatic no. Well, he could take a running jump. She would not date Andreas again!

She waited until the burning in her cheeks had died down

and then walked back into the dining room, meeting Jill's inquiringly raised eyebrows with a careful smile. 'It was Andreas,' she said quietly, noticing the way Dimitra and Evangelos froze momentarily before they carried on eating.

'Oh, yes?' Jill had never been renowned for her tact, but Sophy had been hoping for once her sister might be a little diplomatic. It wasn't to be. 'Why was he calling you?'

'Just to say he had to go to Athens on business,' Sophy said a trifle limply, hoping it might encourage Jill to be subtle as she made her voice as dismissive as she could.

'Oh, yes, the Tripolos contract. You remember I told you about it, my dear?' Evangelos was talking to his wife but Sophy suspected it was more to save her further embarrassment than anything else, especially when he turned to include Jill and Sophy as he said, 'Andreas is a brilliant businessman. I would be lost without him, but sometimes I feel he works too hard.'

'That is because there is no one to encourage him home at night,' Dimitra said maternally. 'He needs a wife. I have told him this many times. It is high time he settled down.'

'Perhaps that is why he has not looked for one?' Evangelos returned with a wry smile and raised eyebrows.

'He thinks I am a fussy mother.' There was no rancour in Dimitra's voice and her eyes were full of love as she looked at her husband. 'But I know my Andreas. He will never be content with the beautiful, mindless creatures who throw themselves at him and have nothing in their heads but cotton wool. Nevertheless, he does need a wife, the right sort of girl.'

Dimitra's voice was light and her gaze was steady as she smiled at them all, but as they continued to eat Sophy felt Andreas's mother had been saying much more than the mere words indicated. Dimitra didn't think that she was making a play for Andreas, did she? Sophy asked herself in horror, nearly choking on a piece of green pepper as the thought hit and hastily taking a sip of wine.

Had Dimitra been trying to tactfully warn her off without saying anything direct? It might indeed look as though she had thrown herself at Andreas as far as his parents were concerned, considering he had taken her out to dinner last night and she hadn't got home to the early hours. What would they say if they knew he had asked her out tomorrow night?

She wriggled uncomfortably in her seat and found she had no appetite for the mouthwatering array of desserts Ainka brought in after the little maid had cleared away the other dishes.

Andreas clearly conducted his life independently of his parents, and that was fine—to be expected in a man of his age—but considering she was here as Evangelos and Dimitra's guest, she was in a totally different position.

She sipped her coffee thoughtfully, joining in the conversation with the others automatically but with her mind a million miles away as she considered how best to get a message to Andreas the next day to emphasise she definitely, *definitely* had no intention of seeing him on a one-to-one basis again.

Dimitra suggested they might like to have coffee on the patio again, the night being a humid one, and as they all rose to walk out into the scented night air Sophy felt a restraining hand on her elbow. 'Sophy?' Dimitra's voice was low as Jill and her husband disappeared out of the dining room doors, the long silky curtains billowing a little behind them.

'Yes?' Sophy forced a smile to her face as she waited for the polite cautionary word about Andreas she was sure would follow. She didn't blame Dimitra; one son had married an English girl and had been lost to her for ever, so it was only natural Dimitra would prefer Andreas to marry what she was sure his parents would describe as a 'good Greek girl', someone familiar with their culture and on their wavelength. Which meant any involvement, however transitory, with Jill's sister was not to their liking.

'Andreas wants to see you again, doesn't he?' It was a statement of fact, and followed by a little rush of words as Dimitra said, 'Oh, forgive me, my dear, for speaking to you in this way about a matter which is of no concern of mine, but I feel I just wanted to tell you...'

'Yes?' Sophy wasn't quite sure where Dimitra was coming from. There was none of the gentle aggression she had expected.

'He is not an island, although I know he gives that impression,' Dimitra said softly, embarrassment making her colour high. 'To the outside world he is Andreas Karydis, virtual head of a vast shipping empire which he controls by being hard, ruthless and clever. He has an intuitive knowledge of people which he uses to his advantage, but that has made him very cynical for one so young. He is not a fool, in other words.'

'I think I realised that in the first five minutes I met him,' Sophy said quietly. No one could think Andreas a fool.

'He likes you.' Dimitra's soft gaze was very steady, and Sophy suddenly realised Andreas's mother was made of sterner stuff than she had thought. 'And he doesn't like many people, I'm afraid. Oh, he will use them—the women too, if they are foolish enough to throw themselves at him—but he never allows anyone to touch the man inside. And the man inside is a good man. Of course, I am his mother and so I must confess to being biased. But I know he needs peace and happiness like everyone else.'

'Dimitra, I'm not looking for any sort of relationship at the moment,' Sophy said softly. Especially with Andreas. But she couldn't very well say that to his mother. And she wasn't quite sure about the liking part, either; she and

Andreas struck sparks off each other and there was no doubt the physical chemistry was there, but as for liking her... But she couldn't say that either—that it was good old-fashioned lust that attracted him.

Dimitra nodded slowly. 'I think I knew this. But...' She shrugged in a very continental way and didn't continue what she had been about to say. 'No matter.' She smiled at Sophy. 'You will not tell Andreas I have spoken to you in this way? He would be most annoyed with me.'

'Of course not.' Sophy still wasn't a hundred per cent sure exactly what way Andreas's mother had spoken! She rather suspected Dimitra had been trying to find out how her daughter-in-law's sister felt about becoming one of Andreas's 'women', and Sophy could well imagine there had been a velvet-coated warning in Dimitra's comment about women who were foolish enough to throw themselves at Andreas. And she didn't doubt there had been plenty.

Which made Sophy all the more surprised with herself when—she and Dimitra having started to walk across the room to join the other two outside, and Dimitra asking in a low undertone if she was going to see Andreas again—she answered in the affirmative. 'Tomorrow night,' she said quietly. 'He has asked me to have dinner with him. He's picking me up at six o'clock.'

Sophy determined she was not going to agonise over what to wear this time when, later the next afternoon, she emerged from the shower and stood in front of her wardrobe gazing at the clothes she had brought with her. She lifted a simple, pastel blue dress with an asymmetric hemline off one of the hangers and laid it on the bed, along with a cotton cardigan in the same colour. Decision made, she told herself firmly.

She dried her hair, applied her make-up and was ready

to go and sit with Jill and Michael at half-past five, Michael being in the process of munching his way through his tea on the patio.

'Very nice.' Jill smiled at her with her mouth but Sophy noticed her sister's eyes were troubled. 'You look lovely.'

'What's the matter?' Sophy asked directly.

'The matter? Nothing. Of course nothing's the matter,' Jill returned brightly, and then, as Sophy's wry expression didn't change, Jill said quietly, 'Don't get in too deep, Sophy. He is Theodore's brother, remember.'

It was said discreetly, in an expressionless voice, with Michael in mind, and Sophy's voice was equally flat when she replied, 'Half-brother, Jill. They only share the same mother, remember, and Dimitra is a love,' even as she asked herself why on earth she was defending Andreas. 'And Evangelos's a nice man.'

'Oh, I know, Evangelos and Dimitra are lovely but—'

Jill stopped abruptly, shaking her head as though she didn't know how to express her misgivings, and Sophy caught one of her sister's hands. 'Don't worry.' She squeezed Jill's hand very slightly. 'It's just dinner and he knows the score. I've made it abundantly clear I'm not looking for romance. He's not my type.'

'Andreas doesn't fit into a type,' Jill murmured ruefully.

The two women stared at each other for a moment, but there was no time for further confidences as the next instant a deep, dark voice from somewhere inside the house proclaimed the subject of their conversation had arrived early and Sophy's heart jumped.

She resisted the impulse to jump to her feet, rising slowly as she said goodbye and walking calmly through the open doors into the dining room, whereupon she made her way into the hall where Andreas was standing talking to Evangelos about a business matter, from what she could determine, before he looked up and saw her.

Her heart was thudding fit to burst but she looked cool and contained to the big dark man watching her so intently, his eyes narrowing slightly as he took in the gleaming silk of her hair and the classically casual simplicity of the sleeveless, fitted dress and matching peep-toe court shoes.

Evangelos made his goodbyes and exited via where Sophy had come from, presumably to see Jill and his grandson, leaving the two of them standing in a pool of sunlight in the hall.

'I missed you yesterday,' Andreas murmured softly, lifting a hand and tracing the outline of her small jaw with one finger.

He was wearing a beautifully tailored summer suit in pale grey, his white shirt and grey tie of the same expensive silk, and looked every bit the powerful wealthy tycoon.

Sophy blinked, the reality of him a hundred times more disturbing than all her thoughts over the last twenty-four hours. 'You barely know me,' she said as steadily as her racing heart would allow, 'so how could you possibly miss me?'

'Time's relative,' he replied, pinning her with his lethal dark gaze. 'How else can you explain the fact that you can know some people all your life and their impact on you barely touches the surface, whereas others...' He smiled slowly. 'Others become important within minutes.'

She didn't know how to answer that and so she said nothing, and after a moment or two he slanted a look at her under half-closed lids as he said, 'All ready? Goodbyes said?'

He made it sound as if she was leaving for good, and to bring things back into line with how she saw the evening progressing, Sophy said quietly but firmly, 'I can't be late again, Andreas. It isn't fair on the rest of the household.'

He looked hard at her and then glanced down at her feet. 'Where are they?' he asked in tones of great surprise.

'What?' She followed his gaze to her feet.

'The glass slippers. Isn't that what Cinderella wore?' he asked blandly, his eyes glinting his amusement. 'But don't worry, Cinders. You will go to the ball.'

'Very funny.' But she couldn't help laughing.

He took her hand, grinning at her as he said, 'Come on, woman, I haven't got time to bandy words with you. I'm hungry.'

Once out on the driveway Sophy was surprised to see a low, lean sports car crouching in front of them. 'Where's Paul?' she asked quickly. Three was safer than two by a long chalk.

'I don't use Paul all the time. I drove myself to the airport yesterday and I only got back an hour or two ago, so…' He waved his hand at the sleek silver beast in front of them. 'I'm quite a good driver,' he assured her modestly. 'Don't worry.'

She didn't doubt it, but the car was a sex machine with two low front seats and a powerful long bonnet and little else. It was not how she had envisaged the evening beginning.

Sophy gritted her teeth and allowed him to help her into the passenger seat, whereupon she had the uncomfortable feeling she was at eye level with the road. The inside was all leather, with a dashboard that looked like it had come out of a Bond film, and when Andreas slid in beside her she realised he was close. Very close. She swallowed hard and forced herself not to fidget.

The engine growled into life and the beast leapt down the driveway. 'Where…where are we going?' she managed as they exited through the gates, her stomach feeling as though it had been left behind on the drive. 'Is it far?' She hoped not.

'Surprise.' It was cool and laconic and she instantly bristled.

'I don't like surprises.'

'Force yourself,' he said pleasantly.

She gave up at that point. It was quite enough to try and keep body and soul together in this monster of a machine, especially with Andreas sitting so close she couldn't have put a pin between them, and his firm strong hands gripping the leather steering wheel on the perimeter of her vision as she stared goggle-eyed out of the massive windscreen.

Andreas drove like he lived, fast and ruthlessly, and more than once Sophy found herself praying that if—*if*—they reached their destination in one piece by some miracle, she would insist on a taxi home. Formula One was all very well but not her scene!

It was some ten minutes before she realised she had relaxed and was actually enjoying the ride, and as she cast a sidelong glance at Andreas she saw the hard firm mouth twitch slightly. 'Okay?' he murmured mockingly, his expression making it quite clear he had been aware of her nervousness and moreover had enjoyed it. 'The first time is not always the best.'

Barbarian. And he needn't think she was going to respond to the double meaning she knew full well he intended in that enigmatic sentence, either. 'I'm fine,' she said brightly. 'Are we nearly there?' Wherever there was.

'Another few minutes.'

It was another ten, but then the car was nosing its way quietly through automatic gates which closed soundlessly behind them and growling gently up a slight, tree-bordered incline to come to rest in front of a long, low, sprawling villa of mellow honey-coloured stone, its red tiled roof dappled by sunlight.

'This is your home,' Sophy accused uncertainly. 'Isn't it?'

Andreas cut the engine, settling back in his seat as he draped one arm round the back of hers. 'Do you mind?' he drawled easily. 'It's been a long forty-eight hours and I need to shower and change and relax. Paul's wife cooks better than any chef I know so you'll have a good dinner.'

'Paul and his wife live with you?' It reassured her fractionally. But only fractionally. This was the wolf's lair.

'They have their own separate annexe at the side of the house,' he assured her gently, having to go and spoil the moment by adding, his voice mocking, 'so you'll be quite safe, Cinders.'

'I never thought otherwise.' She glared at him, her angry irritation at his easy reading of her mind not helped by the wicked glitter in his dark eyes as he left the car.

'Little liar.'

She ignored that, trying to scramble out of the car, only to realise she needed the assistance of the hand he'd put out to help her, his eyes moving appreciatively over the length of golden tanned skin her skirt was revealing. By the time she was standing on the pebbled drive, her cheeks were as red as the full-blown, scarlet roses draping the arched porch.

The villa was completely concealed from the road by trees, but as Sophy turned to look fully at it she caught a glimpse of vivid blue beyond, the scent of roses, grass and sea combining to make her say, her eyes wide, 'Your house overlooks the sea?'

'Yes. The garden runs down to the beach,' he said lazily.

'How wonderful.' She had always adored the sea.

'Come and see for yourself.' He took her arm as the front door opened and a small, squat woman came waddling forward to meet them, the equally small figure of Paul just behind his wife, and after brief introductions Andreas led her into the house.

It was all wood floors and exquisite rugs, with an air of spaciousness and comfort that sat well with the big plump sofas and modern furnishings. There were five bedrooms complete with en-suites upstairs, Andreas informed her, and downstairs the space was divided into a large study, cloakroom, kitchen, breakfast and dining room, with a wonderful sitting room overlooking the beautiful three-tiered gardens which were enormous and, true to Andreas's word, ran right down to a beach of white sand.

Just outside the sitting room, which had one wall of glass inset with big glass doors to take in the magnificent view, shallow stone steps led down to the first tier of the garden which was pebbled and surrounded on three sides by feathered ferns and flowered bushes in great earthenware pots, in the middle of which sat several tables and chairs and upholstered loungers. More steps led down to the next two tiers of lawns embowered with vegetation, and then there was only an endless sweep of sand and blue sea beyond.

Cypresses flanked the sides of the garden and the scent of myriad blossoms was heavy and sweet, vying with the distinctive salt of the sea. The flowers and trees and green grass, the whiteness of the sand beyond and the dazzling blue of the sea in the clear, hard light was breathtaking, the sea appearing to be a flat shimmering sheet of blue watered silk.

'Beautiful, is it not?' Andreas spoke softly at the side of her, his eyes on her entranced gaze.

'Incredible,' she agreed faintly. Paradise on earth.

'There is only the occasional property dotted here and there along the coastline,' Andreas said quietly, 'and the beach is always empty. You can imagine you are the only person alive in all the world down there, and you never see another soul.'

'Hence the skinny-dipping?' It was out before she thought about it but she'd instantly imagined him cutting through the water.

He smiled, a slow, sexy smile. 'Hence the skinny-dipping,' he agreed softly. And then he bent and kissed her, a light, skimming kiss that nevertheless sent frissons of pleasure into every nerve and sinew. He smelt of the flowers and the sea and sunshine, and something else. Something very male and heady that curled her toes in her smart shoes and made her want to run her hands over his hard, broad shoulders and tangle her fingers in his hair, tugging his mouth closer and closer.

'Come and sit down and Alethea will bring you a drink,' Andreas said easily as he led her down the steps to a table and chairs shaded by the feathered leaves of a jacaranda. 'As well as being my driver, Paul makes the best cocktail you will ever taste, and at this time of the evening, after the sort of day I've had, nothing else will do. I won't be long.'

And so she sat in the captivating surroundings, her eyes roaming over the hypnotisingly lovely view as she soaked up the warmth and pungent, exotic perfume of the vegetation and sipped Paul's cocktail, which was as delicious as Andreas had promised.

Andreas joined her after a few minutes, his damp hair curling slightly on to his brow. It gave the hard, handsome face a touch of boyishness that was dynamite, and it took a moment or two for Sophy to be able to say, her tone airy, 'Enjoy your shower?' while she pulled herself together.

'Heaven.' He smiled at her, his tone easy.

He'd changed into a short-sleeved charcoal shirt and black jeans after the shower and he looked devastatingly attractive. Sophy's gaze jerked away from his to conceal the rush of sexual hunger that had taken her completely unawares, and she took a hasty sip of the cocktail, needing the Dutch courage.

Andreas stretched out long legs with a sigh of contentment, draining his glass in a couple of swallows and refilling it from the cocktail shaker he had brought out with him. After one long swallow he placed his glass on the table at the side of him and shut his eyes, his face raised to the sun. 'I want you to let me show you a little of my country while you are here,' he said quietly without moving. 'Some of ancient Greece.'

She glanced at the strong lean body and chiselled face, noticing how thick his eyelashes were as they rested on the tanned skin of his face, and her voice was a little throaty as she said, 'That's very kind, but it's not necessary.'

'Don't be so English.' It was mild but Sophy wasn't fooled by his relaxed manner. 'There are some wonderful sights not too far away, and it would only mean us staying overnight once or twice in the odd place. Thessaloniki has a superb museum holding the gold of King Philip, and at Pella there is the birthplace of Alexander the Great, and the earliest mosaics in Greece. You can't leave Greece without visiting the Acropolis and Mount Olympus, and there's the rock formations of Meteora and much more all within driving distance.'

Sophy hadn't heard anything more after the staying overnight bit. She drew a deep breath and said quietly, 'That's impossible and you know it. I couldn't possibly take off with you anywhere.'

'Why? You wanted me to tell you about Greece. I'm showing you instead, which is far better,' he said reasonably, 'now isn't it?'

'Not with Jill to consider, not to mention your work.'

He opened his eyes and sat up straighter. 'I'm the boss; I can take a few days holiday if I like,' he said mildly, 'and I know for a fact that Jill and Michael have been invited on a trip on Stevos's parents's yacht. If Jill knows that you will be otherwise occupied, she wouldn't feel so bad about leaving you.'

'Jill didn't say anything to me about a trip.' Sophy felt ridiculously hurt that Andreas knew more than she did.

'Perhaps because she doesn't know yet,' Andreas

drawled lazily, 'but Stevos's father works for me and he told me what he had in mind. I thought it was an excellent idea.'

Sophy stared at him. If it wasn't the height of presumption, she could almost imagine that Andreas had put Stevos's father up to this, but that was too ridiculous. He wouldn't do all that just to be with her. 'Whatever, I couldn't possibly just take off with you,' she repeated firmly. 'You know I couldn't.'

He sent her a mildly amused smile that didn't reach his eyes. 'You could do exactly that,' he argued gently.

'Whatever would your parents think?'

'That I was being the perfect host?' he suggested softly.

'Ha!' She glared at him, hardly able to believe he was serious.

Andreas considered her for another moment. 'Is that rather cryptic exclamation supposed to mean something?' he asked at last.

He was being purposely obtuse. 'You know exactly what it means,' Sophy fumed, swigging the last of her cocktail in her anger, and ignoring the warning the fuzziness in her head was trying to give her regarding the potency of Paul's cocktails. 'It would look as if—' She stopped abruptly, seeing that the amusement had now crept into his eyes and that his firm mouth was twitching slightly. He was laughing at her! She gritted her teeth and continued, 'As if we were more than just friends.'

'Separate rooms, I promise.' He surveyed her from under dark brows. 'And I'll make that clear to everyone, although why on earth two adults of our age have to answer to anyone but ourselves beats me,' he finished as though she was being unreasonable.

'Because I'm not like that and I don't want your parents to get the wrong idea,' she hissed tightly. 'I wouldn't dream of going to bed with someone I hardly know.'

'Exactly.' His smile was as sharp as a knife. 'And the best way to get to know someone is to spend time with them, right? We'll explore together, eat together, be together. No strings attached and strictly on your terms. You are Jill's sister, Michael is our shared nephew, so we owe it to them to be nice to each other, yes?'

'That's the worst line I've heard yet.' She scowled at him to prevent her lips twitching with amusement at his transparent hypocrisy. 'I can't believe you'd use an innocent little boy to get your own way.'

'Neither can I,' he said with a remarkable lack of remorse. 'It just shows me what lengths you've driven me to. You ought to be ashamed of yourself,' he added reprovingly.

'Me?' There was no way, no way on earth she would agree to such a crazy, dangerous suggestion. 'Me ashamed of myself?'

'Say you will come, Sophy.' He'd risen swiftly to his feet, pulling her up with him, and as always his accent gave her name a sensuousness an English voice couldn't hope to achieve. He kissed her, hard and long and very completely, and by the end of it her breath was shuddering and her legs were fluid. The heat of the sun was warm now rather than hot, the fierceness of the day mellowing to a delicious caress, and overhead a lone gull wheeled and circled in the air currents calling its melancholy cry to the wind. Nothing seemed real any more, only Andreas...

'Just a few days out of real life,' he whispered coaxingly against her mouth, teasing her with his tongue. 'A golden time to remember.' His hands came up to frame her face and they were gentle, incredibly gentle for such a big man. 'It will be good.'

He kissed her again, tasting and teasing until she kissed him back, and then his hands followed the smooth line of her throat, over the soft swell of her breasts where they lingered to caress the peaks into tortured life before continuing to the narrow span of her waist. 'Just a few days,' he murmured again.

He kept the pace slow, kissing her deeply one moment and then returning to cover her forehead, her temples, her eyelids, her cheekbones in hot little burning kisses that made her mouth search for his long before he assuaged its hunger once again.

The blood was surging through her veins now in a riot of sensation, the scent of him all about her as his lips and his hands continued to work their magic.

She could feel him trembling as he pulled her hard into the length of him, the kiss suddenly deepening into sheer hot and heady passion as she felt the power of his arousal against her softness. And then, almost as though he had recognised his control was slipping, he moved her away from him slightly, kissing her hard one last time before he said, 'Say yes, Sophy.'

She opened heavy lids, shattered and breathless by the flood of feelings he'd ignited and her head whirling. 'Andreas—'

'Say yes,' he commanded again, his dark eyes glittering as they looked down into her flushed face. 'Nothing will happen that you do not want, I promise you this.'

'You promise?' Her eyes were still dilated with desire. 'Separate rooms and nothing heavy?'

'If that is what you want.'

'It is.'

'Then so be it.'

And it was done.

CHAPTER EIGHT

'YOU'VE done *what*?'

Jill's voice was a screech and not at all like its normal soft self. Sophy stared at her sister, glad she'd waited to tell her about her trip with Andreas when they were alone. Dimitra and Evangelos had taken their grandson to visit some friends who ran riding stables, but Jill—who preferred her horses in fields at a safe distance and had no interest in equine pursuits—had opted to stay at the villa.

'I've said I'll go on a little sight-seeing trip with him for a couple of days,' Sophy repeated flatly. 'That's all. And I've made it clear it's not a Mr and Mrs Jones thing, if that's what's bothering you. He's booking separate rooms.'

'I can't believe I'm hearing this. Is it the sun, or what? Something's addled your brain.' Jill stared at her, her eyes wide.

Sophy had been thinking the same thing herself, right from the moment the limousine had dropped her home the night before and she had watched it draw away, Andreas's big figure next to Paul's suddenly becoming that of a near stranger again. But it hadn't felt like that when she had been with him at his home. The whole evening had been wonderful, magical, and the full enormity of what she had promised had only hit when she had stood by herself on the steps watching the car move away.

'I mean, you've always been the one who's tried to stop me doing daft things,' Jill continued plaintively. 'This just isn't like you, Sophy. And with Andreas, of all people.'

No, it wasn't like her. Sophy tried to quell the panic that had been churning her stomach at intervals ever since she had sat in her room last night. She had only managed a couple of hours' sleep. 'It's just a couple of days,' she repeated, as much for her benefit as Jill's. 'It doesn't mean anything.'

'I'm sure it doesn't, not to Andreas.' And then, as Sophy winced visibly, Jill said quickly, 'Oh, I'm sorry, sis, I am really, but I don't want you getting hurt. Andreas is... Well, he's just one of those men who's got everything, isn't he? And the women love him. He's more than able to look on this as a little flirtation and no doubt he's expecting you to do the same. A good time had by both and no regrets sort of approach. But you aren't like that. The trouble is...'

'What?' As Jill's voice trailed away, Sophy repeated, 'What were you going to say?'

'The trouble is, you look so different on the outside to how you are on the inside,' Jill said woefully, suddenly reaching out and clasping her sister's hands in her own. 'I didn't realise it when we were younger. I took you completely for granted, I suppose, but the way Mum was and us never knowing him, our father—' neither Jill or Sophy had ever been able to bring themselves to use the more familiar term of 'dad' '—affected you much more than it did me. You used to look after me, shield me from so much, but the consequences of all that mean you're—'

'What?' Sophy said again. 'Come on, Jill. Spit it out.'

'Damaged,' Jill said reluctantly, waiting for the blast.

'Damaged?' Now it was Sophy's turn to show outrage. 'Excuse me, but hold your horses here, Jill.' She wrenched her hands away, standing up and moving away from the patio where the two of them had been enjoying morning elevenses in the sunshine, before turning and facing her sister again, her face scarlet.

'I am most certainly not damaged,' she bit out firmly, 'and if anyone but you had had the cheek to say that they'd have had a good slap. I can't believe you've been thinking that about me.'

'Sophy, listen to me.' In her agitation Jill was wringing her hands, and as though suddenly becoming aware of it she placed them palm down on the top of the patio table. 'I'm not criticizing you, far from it, but you need to have everything in order in your life; you always have done. You have to be in control.'

'That's not a crime,' Sophy shot back quickly, 'or a personality defect. In fact, most people would look on it as an asset, if anything. It's got me a great job, anyway, now hasn't it?'

'And men?' Jill said very quietly. 'You've always gone for the easy-going, academic type. Impractical in the main, quiet, certainly unassuming. Nice, caring sort of men.'

'So?' Sophy glared at her. 'There's nothing wrong with that, either?'

'So you can't put Andreas in that category, not remotely.'

They stared at each other for a full minute before Sophy retraced her steps and sat down again, taking a long gulp of coffee. 'I know that,' she said more quietly. 'I do *know* that.'

'It's obvious there's something there between you; it has been from day one,' Jill said softly at the side of her. 'Even his parents recognised it. But whereas for Andreas this has probably happened—' She stopped abruptly, colouring slightly.

'Hundreds of times?' Sophy put in tightly. 'Is that it?'

'Well, yes. But you aren't like him. They don't know you like I do, and I know that for you to be like you are he's touched something deep inside. He'll hurt you, devastate you, and he won't even know, Sophy. Don't you *see*? He won't even realise.'

Sophy listened numbly to her own subconscious fears

being spoken out loud. She didn't try to argue with Jill any more because she knew her sister was only speaking the truth.

This fierce attraction she had for Andreas *was* something outside her understanding, and it frightened her as much as it thrilled. Even last night, when she had been wrapped in the magic he had created, she had been aware of the danger. Perhaps that was part of it—a sort of crazy rebellion against all the years of conforming? Most teenagers had their insurrectionary stage but she had never been able to indulge in such a luxury.

'If I say I know you are right and that I'll make very sure not to get involved, does that help?' she said after a few moments. 'If I promise to keep him at arm's length?'

'It does if I can be sure you really mean it and you aren't just saying it to make me feel better,' Jill said in true blunt sisterly fashion. 'But I've seen the way you look at each other.'

'I mean it.' Sophy raised her head and looked into the mirror image facing her with such concern. 'I promise. The thing is, I want to go, Jill. I've never felt so alive as I've felt the last few days and I want to have some fun, for once. I won't do anything silly, and Andreas knows I've got no intention of sleeping with him, but I just want to be with him for a while.'

'If that was supposed to make me feel better, it doesn't,' Jill said ruefully.

'Best you're going to get.' Sophy forced a quick grin. 'So, you'll be getting an invitation to go lording it on Stevos's father's yacht, and I'll be touring the country with one of its most eligible males. We never dreamt of that when we were sitting on the plane coming over, did we?'

'Oh, Sophy.' Jill's voice was troubled. 'Be careful.'

Two days later, when Sophy emerged into bright sunshine with her overnight case crammed to bursting, she glanced across the drive to where Andreas was sitting waiting for her in the sports car, the roof rolled back and his black hair shining in the white light. He looked every inch an icon of the silver screen.

She must be mad. The same thought had occurred at five-minute intervals all during the last forty-eight hours, but since talking to Jill a number of things had clarified in her mind.

Like Andreas himself had said, this would be a few days out of real life—a golden time to remember. She didn't intend to treat it anymore seriously than he did. She was physically attracted to him and she had to admit she liked his company—when he wasn't being confrontational and difficult, that was—but now she had acknowledged both those things she was in a position of control again. He knew the score, she hadn't tried to mislead him in any way—just the opposite—and he was quite prepared to accept this wasn't going to be a full-blown affair in the physical sense. She'd been totally up front and honest.

Anyway... She smiled at him as he raised a lazy hand in greeting. He probably secretly felt it was the best thing all round. With Jill being an in-law, it wasn't the most sensible thing in the world to have a fling with her sister. Too messy and potentially problematical, and she knew from little remarks Dimitra had let drop over the last few days that Andreas ran his life with a ruthless uncomplicatedness.

Yes, she could handle this. She could. But she was still probably mad! But a little summer madness was excusable, wasn't it?

The morning air was warm and moist, the sun blazing down out of a crystal blue sky, and as Sophy ran lightly over to the car Andreas slid out of the driver's seat and opened the small boot for her case.

'Good morning.' He kissed her full on the mouth before stepping back a pace, his eyes roaming over her clear creamy skin and blonde hair. She was wearing white cotton trousers and a white silk top and no make-up, and didn't look a day over twenty-one. 'You look like the essence of summer.'

'Do I?' She grinned back at him, determined to start as she meant to carry on and keep things light and amusing. She let her eyes run over the big muscled body clothed in black denim shirt and jeans, and wrinkled her smooth nose consideringly. 'You don't,' she pronounced at last, slanting a mocking glance out of blue eyes.

'Thank goodness for that. In the car, wench.'

That conversation set the tone for the most deliriously happy few days of Sophy's life. Andreas knew the surrounding country like the back of his hand and the first morning they went straight to Thessaloniki, Greece's second city, where they visited the Acropolis and Sophy stood spellbound by the panoramic view, before they paid a visit to the gold of King Philip.

They ate lunch mid afternoon in a tiny inn perched high on a flower-covered hillside, before continuing on to Pella where they browsed in the museum for a while along with seeing the superb ancient mosaics. It was fascinating and enthralling and slightly eerie.

Andreas took her to a small sweet little café with tiny carved wooden balconies and white-painted walls after they had emerged into languid evening sunshine, and they sat watching the world go by while drinking rich red wine and eating *keftedes* and warm garlic bread at a little table outside.

The evening sky was full of muted colours flowing into a lake of gold by the time they left, and they wandered through dusky streets where the odd intermittent barking of a dog or once, the unmistakable sound of a bonzouki could be heard. It was peaceful and timeless and possessed of a charm that couldn't be translated into words.

Their hotel was a modern one and, true to his word, Andreas left her at the door to her room, kissing her very thoroughly before he left. It took her a long time to get to sleep.

And so one golden day followed another. They talked and they laughed together, touched and tasted each other, but all within the constraints Sophy had set. She felt she had got to know Andreas better than she had ever known anyone in her life and, perversely, in the same breath, that the more she got to know him the less she seemed to understand.

When he suggested on the afternoon of the third day that they spend a couple of more days together she didn't object, dutifully phoning Jill to explain and to ask her sister how she and Michael had enjoyed the yacht, and then returning to the car and to Andreas with the others wiped clear from her mind the moment she put the telephone down.

They visited the spectacular Byzantine monasteries perched high on the cliffs at Meteora, the olive groves of Amphissa and much, much more, but on the night of the fourth day Sophy cried long and hard once she was alone in her hotel room.

Perhaps it was just that the idyll had ended and they had to go back to the real world the next day? she asked herself flatly, when—at two in the morning and utterly unable to sleep—she stepped on to the balcony of her small hotel room and sat looking out over quiet streets sleeping under a calm, deep midnight-blue sky pierced with stars. And soon she would be back in England, back in the frantic pace of life that she had thought she loved but which now seemed so far away.

Why hadn't Andreas tried to make love to her? The thought she had been ignoring for the last two or three days wouldn't be denied any more. She hadn't expected he would be so crass for the first twenty-four hours or so, and she knew she had *told* him this trip had to be a platonic one, but why hadn't he pushed things? He was that sort of man, wasn't he? The sort that took what he wanted, regardless of anyone else? Wasn't he?

Of course, she would have fought him and made it clear an affair wasn't on the cards, but she didn't understand this...control. It could only mean he had mastered the feeling he had had for her. And yet the way he kissed her, the way he held her *wasn't* platonic. She had expected him to try and cajole her, to use his infinite experience to sweep her off her feet—something! But he wasn't conforming to the mental summing up she had made of him before the trip.

She frowned to herself, her face feeling tight after the tears she had shed earlier and her mind in turmoil. There had been Jill warning her to be on her guard before she had left, and Andreas hadn't put a foot out of place. It would be funny if it wasn't so humiliating. And she did feel humiliated...and hurt, which was utterly unreasonable, of course. She ought to be glad he'd kept to their bargain. It had saved any unpleasantness and meant they could part as friends when she left for England.

Andreas was in the room next to her; what would he say if she knocked on his door and asked to go in? She had had the odd crazy thought like this one over the last few days—impulses to reach up and tug his mouth down to hers at the strangest moments, or suddenly throw herself into his arms and ask him to make love to her. Impulses she'd denied, but which refused to lie down and die. It was high time she was back at the villa with Jill and Michael. She nodded silently at the thought. Andreas had exploded into her life with all the dark force of a nuclear missile and embedded himself deep in her psyche. No one had ever affected her like this and she didn't recognise herself any more.

She shivered, although the night was warm and humid, and stepped back into the bedroom. She was just about to close the balcony windows when she heard the ones next door flung open.

A single thickness of white-painted brickwork on both sides of the balcony gave the rooms privacy, but she could distinctly hear Andreas sigh as he sat down on one of the wicker chairs the balconies contained, and then she heard the chink of a glass.

He couldn't sleep, either. She wouldn't have believed how comforting the thought was as a little tingle of something like excitement slid down her spine and her heart began to pound. Perhaps he was thinking of her? Maybe his body and mind were as restless as hers—knowing full well what was needed to assuage the craving that was part pain, part pleasure.

Should she call out softly to him? Suggest they share a nightcap together as they were both awake? And if by any chance one thing led to another—well, it wasn't a crime, was it? She wanted him, needed him, tonight. She ached for his touch.

The sudden realisation of where her mind had gone came like a physical jolt, and it was in that second Sophy realised that much more than her body was involved in her feelings for Andreas. She had fallen for him. Okay, so she wasn't sure if it was love or not—certainly this emotion was as different to the quiet, comfortable contentedness she'd felt with Matthew as it was possible to be—but something in her spirit had been drawn to him from their first meeting and she had started fighting it from that point, too.

'Oh, no...' It was just the faintest of whispers and he couldn't possibly have heard it, but she covered her mouth tightly with the palm of one hand none the less.

Not Andreas Karydis. She couldn't have been so stupid. He was everything she *didn't* like in a man, so how had it happened? He was arrogant and forceful and intensely physical, and in spite of the good time they had had over the last days she didn't doubt for a minute that he could be utterly ruthless and subjective when he had to be. Or when he wanted to be. And he had already made it abundantly clear that he wanted her physically and that was the point of his interest. Dress it up how you like, that was what it boiled down to.

She stepped quietly away from the windows which she left slightly ajar, fearing he would hear if she tried to shut them again, and fumbled among her things for the packet of painkillers she'd brought with her. The weeping she'd indulged in earlier, combined with lack of sleep, had created a nagging ache at the base of her skull, which had got distinctly worse in the last few minutes.

She wasn't going to think about anything any more. She took two of the painkillers with a drink of water and climbed back into bed, drawing the stiff hotel covers over her tense body and willing herself not to cry again. She would be more level-headed in the morning; everything always seemed at its blackest in the hours before dawn.

When Sophy came downstairs in the rather quaint, old-fashioned hotel they had booked into the night before, Andreas was already seated, reading the newspaper, at a table for two in the far corner of the small, flower-festooned dining room. He was sitting next to an open window which overlooked the hotel's pretty cobbled courtyard, which was complete with a sparkling fountain, and for a moment Sophy stood still in the doorway as she looked at him before he became aware of her presence.

The white sunlight picked up a sheen of blue in the jet-black hair and he was frowning slightly as he read, a little habit of his she had noticed over the last few days.

There was something so magnetic about his good looks, his whole persona, she thought weakly. And yet it wasn't really his looks, nor even his powerful body or dark sexiness. She couldn't find words, not even to herself, to explain the age-old call, but it was there, and it was virile and consuming and infinitely dangerous.

Being with him so closely over the last few days had confirmed what she had sensed the first time she'd met him—that women would want him, and badly. He would only have to lift his little finger and they'd come running. To get emotionally involved with a man like him would be a constant agony of wondering. Wondering if one female, more gorgeous or just plain predatory than the rest, had managed to get his attention. Wondering where he was if he was late any time and whether this was the day you would be replaced in his affections. Wondering how long you could hang on to him and to your sanity...

'Miss Fearn?' The young waitress who had served them dinner the night before was at her side, and as Sophy came out of the black thoughts she smiled at the pretty face but didn't correct the girl, letting the Miss ride because it was simpler. Perhaps if you got involved with a man like Andreas you had to let a lot of things ride to keep things simple, she thought bleakly. Other women's come-hither smiles and his responses, a phone call that was supposedly a wrong number, the faint odour of a different perfume to her own or a trace of lipstick...

She had listened to friends and colleagues list all those things during marital or long-term break-ups in her time, and on each occasion she had thought of her mother and the pain her father must have inflicted on a woman whose only mistake was to love her husband utterly. *And whatever her father had had to draw the opposite sex, Andreas had it tenfold.*

She followed the waitress across to the table automatically, forcing a smile as Andreas looked up at their approach. 'What is it? You look pale. Are you unwell?'

He was all concern, but she couldn't keep the thread of stiffness out of her voice as she said, 'No, no I'm all right. I just didn't sleep too well. The bed was lumpy.'

'I told you we should have gone to a more modern hotel, but you insisted you found this one picturesque.'

The tender indulgence with which he spoke was untenable, and her voice was sharp as she said, 'I'm not complaining, merely answering your question.'

Her tone straightened his face and narrowed his eyes, but after a long look at her white complexion he merely said quietly, 'I have waited for you before ordering. I intend to have croissants followed by a full English breakfast. What would you like?'

Sophy glanced up at the waitress. 'Just croissants and coffee for me please.' She had snapped at him and been unforgivably rude; if she hadn't realised it herself the touch of steel in the square jaw would have told her. But this...whatever it was—flirtation, tenuous dalliance, sexual game—had to stop. It had to finish where it mattered, in her head.

She was getting in too deep and Jill had been right after all. He was tying her up in knots and she wasn't even sure if he was aware of it. All she did know was that the more she was with him, the more she fell under his spell, and what would be the outcome? What *could* be the outcome? A brief affair and then a lifetime of regret. He had pursued her because he wanted her physically and she hadn't fallen into his arms like his other women. She appeared unattainable and that had intrigued him.

She remembered her mother saying once, with pathetic

pride, that she had worn her white dress on her wedding day with every right to do so. Whether it had been due to her principles or a strategic plan, her mother had netted her father because she hadn't given him what most other females had been only too ready to give, but it hadn't altered the basic character of the man. Nothing could do that. She'd be fooling herself to think otherwise.

'Okay, what has happened?' Andreas's voice was very quiet.

Sophy glanced at him and found the grey eyes were tight on her face, his own countenance expressionless. She took a deep breath before she could say, 'I don't know what you mean.'

'Don't give me that.' It was low and controlled but intense. 'You are a different woman to the one of the last few days,' he said grimly. 'This Sophy is the one who looked at me with such dislike at the airport, but I thought we had left that behind us.'

'Don't be silly.' Even to herself her voice sounded desperate. 'How could I have looked at you like that when I didn't even know you? And how could anything have happened since last night?'

'This I do not know but I intend to find out,' he said softly.

'There's nothing *to* find out.' This was awful, and it was all her fault. 'You'll just have to take my word on that.'

'So you are the same happy, sparkling-eyed girl of the last few days?' he bit out caustically. 'Is that what you are saying?'

She stared at him miserably. 'It's the end of the sight-seeing,' she said flatly. 'Time to...to get back to normal.'

'Normal?' He flung the paper to one side and leant close to her, taking one of her wrists in his hand as he stopped her instinctive jerk backwards. 'And what is your definition of normal, Sophy? Nothing about this relationship is normal as far as I can see.'

'Please, Andreas.' His fingers were like steel and soon people would begin to notice. 'You're hurting me.'

'Whatever it is that holds you from the past is like a lead weight round your neck,' he grated softly, 'and, believe me, Sophy, it is not normal. You asked me for time and I have given you time, but you are acting as though I forced myself on you last night rather than taking umpteen cold showers and walking the floor until dawn. What the hell do you want from me, anyway?'

'Nothing,' she shot back quickly. 'I want nothing from you. I didn't ask to come on this trip; it was your idea. Remember?'

He let go of her then, settling back in his seat as his eyes continued to hold hers, their grey depths shining silver. 'Yes, I remember,' he said softly after a few seconds had ticked away in a screaming silence that was painful.

The waitress chose that moment to bustle up with coffee and croissants, managing—whether by chance or design—to brush Andreas's shoulder with one ripe breast as she placed their food in front of them. The fact that Andreas didn't appear to notice the manoeuvre was scant comfort to Sophy, and the other woman's actions seemed to confirm everything she was thinking.

'She likes you.' As the waitress disappeared in a flourish of black cotton and lacy white apron, Sophy's voice was very low. Part of her couldn't believe she'd actually said it out loud.

'What?' Andreas had been about to pour them coffee but now he froze, his eyes narrowing still further. 'Who likes me?'

'The waitress,' Sophy said woodenly. 'She likes you.'

'What the hell are you talking about?'

'She wanted you to notice her.'

'Well, I didn't.' He poured two cups of coffee, settled back in his seat again and then stood up, his voice a growl as he said, 'Damn it, I'm not sitting here like this when I want to talk to you, and I sure as hell can't do it in here.'

He pulled her up none too gently and then, despite her protests, all but frogmarched her out of the dining room and out of the hotel into the street outside. He didn't say a word as he whisked her along the pavement to a little dusty square at the end of the street, but after pushing her down on a gnarled wooden bench, sat down beside her. 'I've got the feeling I missed something back there,' he said grimly, 'and I do not like that. Now, explain.'

She stared at him, at the handsome face now set in dark angry lines, at the big broad shoulders and powerful chest, and suddenly wished she was back to yesterday morning when life had been golden.

There was a radio blaring somewhere and a baby crying in the old, gently decaying houses surrounding the square, but apart from a couple of pigeons pecking somewhat lethargically at a piece of stale bread, the place was deserted. 'I want to go back to the hotel,' she said stiffly. 'Right now.'

'Tough.' He eyed her implacably. 'If I'd got what I wanted we would have spent the last four days in bed instead of skirting the issue.' He was clearly determined not to let her off the hook.

'What issue?' She tried not to think about the bed bit.

'You know damn well what issue,' he growled softly. 'The issue of us, and don't say there isn't an us because we wouldn't be here now if there wasn't.'

'There isn't—'

He cut off her voice by the simple expedient of taking her mouth in a kiss that had no gentleness but was all fire and thunder. His lips were urgent and burning as his fingers tangled in her hair, and he crushed her against him almost angrily, forcing her lips apart and exploring her mouth with an arrogance that spoke of possession.

He hadn't kissed her like this before, and although she struggled for a few seconds the swift, hot and insistent flow of desire that immediately scorched her nerve endings was too strong to fight. She wanted him, wanted to be held by him like this.

She fell against him, there in the square in the bright hot sunlight as the kiss deepened still more, his mouth savaging hers, and as always when he so much as touched her the rest of the world faded away.

'*Diabolos.*' It was Andreas who pulled away. 'You say there is no us when I could take you here, now, in the open and you would not resist me?'

Sophy lifted her chin, her heartbeat threatening to choke her as she struggled to control the alien passions his lips and body invoked. 'It was just a kiss,' she said numbly.

He nodded, his eyes merciless. 'But if we had been in your room or mine and I had not stopped, what would it have been then? You want me every little bit as much as I want you, and I am done playing these games. I have been patient and still you fight me, even as your body betrays you every time I touch you. You have been married and so it is not sexual inexperience that holds you back.' He glared at her, his mouth grim.

There was sexual experience and then there was sexual experience, Sophy thought bitterly, and she didn't doubt for a moment she knew none of the tricks and sexual gymnastics a man like Andreas would expect of a woman.

'So, what is it?' he continued relentlessly. 'Why do you continue to fight me and yourself? Are you afraid of me?'

She had to make him see that there could never be anything between them and only the truth—or a limited version of it—would do that. She nerved herself and said quietly, 'Yes.'

His eyebrows rose at the unexpected honesty and he tensed for a moment, before visibly forcing himself to relax and gentling his voice as he said, 'I don't understand, Sophy. Why? What have I done to make you fear me?'

'It's not what you have done.' There was no easy way to say it. 'It's what—who—you are.'

For a moment she was frightened at the look which came over his face, but instead of the explosion she expected his voice was even more controlled when he said coldly, 'Let's take the first definition as the one you really meant, shall we? What, exactly, do you think I am?'

'You…you like women and they like you.' Put like that it sounded ridiculous, and Andreas wasn't slow to capitalise on the fact.

'In other words, I am a normal heterosexual male,' he stated with silky softness. 'Are you telling me this is my crime?'

'No.' She swallowed painfully. He wasn't going to make this easy, but then she hadn't expected him to. 'What I mean is, women will always chase a man like you. There's something about you…' This was going even more badly than she'd feared. 'It's not really your fault,' she finished weakly. 'But I…I don't want to be one of many. Some women can handle that but I can't.'

'Let's get this straight.' His face and body were rigid with rage, only his mouth moved in the carved structure of his countenance and his eyes were as cold and as hard as the rest of him. She didn't recognise the man in front of her as the Andreas she knew, this was a stranger. She could see now how he could effortlessly take over his father's empire and run it even more efficiently than Evangelos; he had only to display a fraction of the ruthlessness that was staring out of his face and any opposition would crumple. He was formidable and she felt scared to death.

'You are saying that I am a philanderer, a womaniser, yes? A Don Juan who keeps his brains in his trousers?'

She flinched a little at the crudity, her eyes opening wide with shock. 'No, no, I'm not saying that.' And she wasn't…was she? She suddenly realised she didn't know what she was saying. 'Just that it would be only natural for you to—'

'Spread myself round a little?' he cut in brutally. Dark colour flared across the hard cheekbones, his grey eyes narrowed and points of steel. 'And you have been thinking this all along, I take it?' he ground out slowly. 'Even the last few days? How charming.'

He was looking at her as though he had never seen her before and now hot panic was surging through her as she realised the enormity of what she had done. She should never have said anything, she told herself wretchedly, but even now a little voice deep within answered, But you had to, you had to. You couldn't have a relationship with a man like Andreas.

'So I am one of those weak and distasteful characters who sleep around and have a different woman for every day of the week?' He rose, staring down into her horrified face with hooded eyes. 'I think we had better get back to the hotel. The sight-seeing, as you pointed out earlier, is over,' he bit out rawly.

'Andreas, don't be like this. Please don't be like this.'

'Like what? Believe me, Sophy, if a man had said half of what you have I would have taken pleasure in rearranging his face. You have labelled me as a stud stallion from the first moment we met and yet you were the one who informed me you do not care for labels.'

The contemptuous statement was nothing less than the truth and his withering scorn brought her shoulders hunching as she too rose from the seat. She had no defence. None.

'Even the worst criminal knows of what he is accused

before he is condemned,' Andreas bit out disgustedly, 'but you sat safe in your little ivory tower and was judge and jury. How many times did I inadvertently say or do something to add weight to my sentence? Did you find it amusing that I was so obviously interested in you? Did you look forward to the moment when you would throw it all back in my face?'

'No!' This had all gone so terribly wrong. 'No, of course not,' she said desperately. 'It wasn't like that. I thought—' What had she thought? She didn't know now. 'I thought we could be friends,' she said helplessly.

'Friends?' He smiled a thin smile that was merely a bitter twisting of his lips. 'There was never any possibility of us being friends, Sophy, so do not lie to yourself. It was always going to be all or nothing.'

He turned from her, leaving her with no choice but to follow him as he walked out of the square and began striding towards the hotel, his body language stating all too clearly he was done with her. She had got what she wanted and she couldn't bear it.

The journey back to Halkidiki was one Sophy wouldn't have wished on her worst enemy. Andreas drove fast and furiously, his face grim and his hands gripping the steering wheel as though he wished it were her neck.

They stopped for lunch in a small town between Dion and Thessaloniki, and after Sophy had tried to apologise and Andreas had cut her off with a voice like ice, she had to force the food past the massive constriction in her throat. She managed it, just, but it sat in her stomach like a stone the rest of the way back to the villa. Which was only what she deserved, she thought.

As they passed through the gates of the estate, the afternoon sun was still high in the sky, and as Sophy saw the familiar building in front of them after they had turned a corner in the long drive she had to fight an absurd desire to cry. She had been so happy when she had left here a few days ago, and now things couldn't be worse. And it was her fault.

'Andreas?' As the car came to a halt she spoke quickly before she lost her nerve. 'I know you are angry with me but could we at least put on some kind of show so as not to upset the others? They won't understand.'

'*I* do not understand,' he shot back violently, before taking an audible breath and flexing his hands on the steering wheel. He breathed deeply once or twice and then said, 'Of course we can be civil, but I think it will be best if I do not trouble you again during the rest of your visit. There are many matters awaiting my attention at work, so this will be quite acceptable.'

He had exited the car before she could say anything more, striding round to the passenger door and helping her out with a formality that made her heart bleed.

Once in the house, Ainka met them in the sunlit hall with the news that the others were out for the day and wouldn't be home until late, and then disappeared upstairs with Sophy's case.

'Thank you for…for showing me around.'

Sophy's voice was small, and Andreas glanced down at her, his face hard. And then he became still when he noticed the tell tale sheen of the tears she was trying to hide. '*Diabolos.*' It was a low muttered oath, and when he took her arm, marshalling her roughly into the dining room and slamming the door behind them, she didn't try to resist.

'This is crazy—you know that, don't you?' His voice was not quiet or conciliatory and the room crackled with tension. 'You insult me and then you look at me the way you did just then. What the hell is the matter with you?'

'Nothing.' All the way home in the car she had been praying for him to give her another chance, to at least let her explain the unexplainable, but now the moment was here all the fears of twenty-eight years rose up in a flood again. She wanted him too much, that was the trouble. She loved him. She had been fighting it for days but now she had to admit it. She loved him in a way she had never loved Matthew, never imagined herself loving, and that made his power over her unthinkable.

'Nothing? You can say nothing?' He gave a harsh bark of a laugh but his voice had been agonised, desperate. 'I touch you and you melt for me—that is not nothing. I do not believe you have ever felt this way before because I know I have not.'

She didn't want to hear this, *couldn't* hear it. She had to believe she was doing the right thing, the only thing.

'Listen to me, Sophy.' He took her arms in his, holding her in front of him as he looked down into her face with burning eyes. 'There was a girl once, many years ago. We were going to be married and then I found out she was playing around. The same old story that happens a hundred times a day. I finished it but I told myself I would never meet anyone else I cared for like I did Larissa. And then I met you and I knew I had never loved her as I was meant to love.'

'No.' Her face was white. 'No, you don't love me.'

'Yes.' He shook her slightly, his body rigid. 'I've had relationships since Larissa but I have always known, and the women have too, that they couldn't go anywhere. But this is different.'

'You thought you loved Larissa but now you say you didn't,' she whispered through pale lips. 'You would say the same to me in time. Someone would come along, someone younger and prettier. And we hardly know each other, anyway,' she finished desperately.

'I have known you from the beginning of time,' he said softly. 'I recognised it that night by the pool, and so did you.'

'No.' She tried to struggle free but he wouldn't let her. 'I don't want this. I don't want you.'

'You want me.' His voice was as hard as steel.

'No.' Fear made her cruel. 'I despise the sort of man you are.'

'Despise me?' His voice was harsh again. 'You couldn't respond like this to a man you despise.'

The kiss was as savagely challenging as his words and continued to be so until she stopped struggling. By the time the force had gone the power of his mouth was holding her more effectively than anything else could have done, and she was accepting his hands and his mouth blindly.

Each one of his kisses was more urgent, deeper, hungrier, and she was answering the desperate need with a desire to match his, passion sending rivulets of sensation into every part of her. His hands had slid under the soft material of her top, sliding over the silky skin beneath as he explored her rounded curves until she moaned beneath his lips.

His tongue was probing, thrusting, sending electric currents coursing through her body as she melted against him, the relentless plundering of her mouth and the sure firm hands on her body creating a throbbing in the core of her that she'd never experienced before. Her body felt hot and molten, and she was no longer sure who was leading and who was following, she just knew she wanted more.

'You see, Sophy?' His voice was shaking, the tremours that pulsed the big male frame echoed in hers. 'You see how it is?'

She couldn't deny the messages her flesh was sending to his, but his voice was a subtle intrusion into the world of colour and light and sensation beneath her closed eyelids, and she opened heavy lids, her mind dizzy.

'This is real,' he said softly. 'I am real. Me, Andreas Karydis. I want you because I love you. Do you understand?'

She wanted to believe him. With all her heart she wanted to believe him but in the final analysis she dared not. She had seen what loving a man with all one's heart and mind and soul and body had done to her mother, and she couldn't cope with that sort of consuming emotion. It had been safe with Matthew; she had been in control and, although life had never been exciting or possessed of highs and lows, it *had* been her life. She had held the strings and kept her autonomy.

And suddenly she saw very clearly what she had to do. Struggling for calmness, she backed away from him, praying she would have the strength to say it all without breaking down.

'I understand,' she said quietly, 'and I love you, too.'

He waited, knowing from the look on her face and the tone of her voice that in spite of her confession something was still terribly, terribly wrong.

'And because I feel like I do, I can't be with you, Andreas.'

He did react then, taking a step towards her which was instantly checked when she said, her hands raised to ward him off, 'Please listen to me. I...I'll try to explain and then you'll see there can't be any sort of future for us.'

She told him it all, starting from the first time, as a small child of perhaps three or four, that she remembered asking about her father. The picture in the attic, her difficult childhood, the heartache and bitterness of spirit that eventually killed her mother, it all came pouring out. 'Jill said something recently that I vehemently objected to,' she finished sadly. 'She said I was damaged. I hated that—it suggests some sort of victim thing—but none the less she's right. I can't change the way I am and all I'd do was to make us both miserable and destroy anything we had, even if—' She stopped abruptly.

'Even if?'

She raised her chin at his soft voice. 'I was going to say even if you are not like my father,' she said jerkily. 'You see, you see how it is? I don't believe you, Andreas. I can't trust you. I care too much to be able to do that. All the time I'd be waiting. No one can live like that.'

She knew from the unmasked agony in the beautiful silver-grey eyes that he knew she meant it. 'So you run back to your insulated little bubble in England, is that it?' he grated. 'Where you consider yourself impregnable. To a life that is risk-free. A life that will eventually dry you up and shrivel everything that makes you you. Fear will turn you into a lonely young woman and then a lonely old one, and it is a poor bedfellow. You have met me now; I shall be there in your head even if you shut me out of your flesh. You can't go back to the way things were before you came here.'

'I can try.' She had to do this for both their sakes, but it was killing her. 'It will be me that suffers, after all.'

'You still don't get it, do you?' He stared at her, his face set and the note of pleading gone from his voice. 'You as an individual finished the day we met. When you suffer, I suffer now. We are in this together. Your pain is my pain, the same as your joy and happiness would be my joy and happiness. Don't you see what you have done, Sophy? You have become part of me and you won't alter that by going away.'

'You'll meet someone else one day.' Even as she said it she knew how trite and insulting it sounded after what he'd just said.

'Thank you.' It was cutting.

Sophy tried to think of something else to say but failed utterly. They remained staring at each other for a moment more before he said, 'Your mind is made up,' and it was a statement of fact, not a question. Nevertheless, she nodded her answer.

He nodded himself, the action curt. 'Goodbye, Sophy.'

'Goodbye.' She felt sick with pain and panic, but deep inside the alternative path—to reach out to him, to say she would love and trust him as he wanted—was as unthinkable as ever.

He gave her one last searching look and then walked across to the door, opening it and passing into the hall beyond without looking back. She heard the front door open and close, and then the roar of the powerful engine on the drive outside.

He had gone. He had left her as she had demanded she be left and he wouldn't try again. Not after all that had been said.

She had got what she wanted and the future couldn't have been more desolate.

CHAPTER NINE

THE rest of the week was torturous but eventually the morning dawned when they were flying home.

Sophy had related the true state of affairs to Jill once her sister had got back to the villa on the day she and Andreas had parted, and Jill had nobly forgone any 'I told you so's', but to Dimitra and Evangelos Sophy had just said she'd enjoyed the sight-seeing trip but Andreas had mentioned he had plenty of work to catch up on. She didn't know if they believed her and she didn't actually care; she was so consumed with misery that, selfishly, nothing else mattered but Andreas.

From a comment dropped at the dinner table the day after she and Andreas had returned from their trip, Sophy learnt from Evangelos that Andreas had flown to America that morning on urgent business and wasn't expected to return for a couple of weeks.

She had been amazed how the news had hit her. The fact that there was no likelihood of seeing him again should have relieved some of her tension and strain, but instead it had sent her falling into a deep well of despair that seemed bottomless.

She combated her wretchedness by forcing herself to appear normal—playing with Michael, chatting to Dimitra and steering the conversation away from Andreas any time she and Jill were alone and her sister tried to bring his name up. She knew Jill meant well and was worried she was bottling all her pain and anguish, but Sophy could no more have discussed the situation than she could have sprouted wings and flown.

Funnily enough, the morning of their departure was a rainy one—the first rain they had seen since landing in Greece. Sophy felt slightly guilty that she welcomed the drizzle but the overcast sky and grey clouds fitted her state of mind much better than the radiantly blue sky and bright sunshine of the previous weeks.

This time it was Evangelos who drove them to the airport, in the prestigious and beautiful Mercedes, much to Michael's delight. The little boy sat at the front with his grandfather and he chattered the whole way to the airport, taking the strain of having to join in any conversation from Sophy who was in the back with Jill. Dimitra had opted to say goodbye at the villa rather than in the cold neutrality of the airport terminal, and she had been weeping as the car had drawn away. However, the fact that Jill had promised to fly out for another visit at Christmas had made her tears not altogether unhappy ones.

Evangelos parked the car and loaded their suitcases on to a trolley, but as the little party made their way into the building he suddenly stopped dead, almost causing Sophy and Jill who had followed behind him and Michael to cannon into his back.

'What on earth…?' they heard him mutter, before he turned round and said, 'Over there, look. It is Andreas, isn't it?'

Sophy looked. It was. An instinctive and primitive fear made her want to run, but she wasn't sure if it was away from him or to him. Instead she just stood absolutely still as she watched him walk towards them. He looked cool and disturbingly calm.

'You're in America,' Evangelos said accusingly.

'Clever me.' Andreas answered his father but his eyes were on Sophy's white, tight face.

'When did you get back?' Evangelos asked bewilderedly. 'And surely the negotiations aren't completed yet?'

'I landed half an hour ago and I fly back in a couple of hours and no, the negotiations aren't complete,' Andreas said expressionlessly. 'However, I've some negotiations of my own which are a damn sight more important. Sophy and I are going for a walk, so you can get the coffees in and we'll see you later.'

'The plane leaves in a couple of hours. Sophy needs to book in,' Evangelos began, but he found he was speaking to thin air, Andreas having taken Sophy's arm and marched her away.

'What…what are you doing?' She found her voice at last but it emerged a shaky whisper.

'Changing schedules, cancelling meetings and flying halfway across the world,' Andreas answered drily without looking down at her. 'Pursuing a woman who has driven me mad from day one.'

He looked every inch the dynamic tycoon in a crisp grey business suit and white shirt, and he took her breath away.

She wasn't aware she was crying until they emerged into the watery sunlight outside, the rain having stopped and a feeble sun beginning to break through the clouds. And then it was Andreas who said very softly, 'Don't cry,' as he reached down and carefully wiped her eyes with a large handkerchief. 'I just needed to see you before you go, that's all. There are things I have to make clear. Things which it's necessary you understand.'

'What things?' They had just turned a corner of the building into a quiet area of reserved parking, and now he stopped, turning her into him and cupping her chin before taking her lips in a hungry kiss, a kiss that was charged with passion and incredibly sweet. It was heaven—and hell—to be in his arms again. Heaven because there was nowhere else she would rather be, and hell because she knew it couldn't last.

'What things?' As he raised his head, she saw his eyes

were very clear and shining silver. 'That I intend to go on doing this, for a start. England is not so very far away and the wonders of modern technology mean I can be with you most weekends.'

It wasn't what she had expected and she stared at him open-mouthed for a moment, before shutting her lips with a little snap. And then she found her voice and said dully, 'You can't.'

'I can.' His voice was exceedingly firm. 'And I'm going to.'

Sophy pushed at his hard chest and felt the steady beat of his heart, but he refused to let her go, even when she said, 'Andreas, this is crazy. I said all there was to say—'

'Exactly.' He reached out and traced the outline of her lips with one finger and she quivered at his touch before she could disguise the weakness. 'You talked, I listened. Now it is my turn. I don't intend to let you ruin both our lives because of a shadowy figure in the past who bears no relation to me,' he said with a touch of grimness. 'I appreciate it might take time to convince you, but we have time. Lots of time.'

'I can't go through all this again. I don't want to talk—'

'I'm talking, you're listening,' he reminded her steadily. 'I've done a lot of thinking while we've been apart, and I can see this has happened too quickly for you, with your childhood and all the baggage you've brought into adulthood. But that *is* how it happens sometimes. My father knew within seconds of meeting my mother that she was the person he wanted to spend the rest of his life with, and nothing could have dissuaded him. I have discovered I am my father's son in more ways than one. I don't intend to give up, Sophy, so face it.'

Sophy shook her head, panic at feeling she was being swept away by an unstoppable force uppermost again. 'Your parents were different,' she objected feverishly.

'That was them, a different situation. You can't relate it to us.'

'I thought there was no us?' And then, as she went to speak, he said softly, 'I am not going to take away your right to choose when you are ready for me, Sophy, not by physical force, or mental. You love me but now you have to get to know me. I understand this. It can be as slow as you want. But please accept this and save us both a lot of wasted time—*I am not going to give up.* Not now, not five or ten or fifteen years from now. You will grow to trust me as well as love me. I want you for my wife, the mother of my children. I want us to grow old together and watch our grandchildren play in the sunshine. Nothing else will do.'

The rush of love she felt was so intense, she had to take a steadying breath before she could say, 'And if it never happens, what then? What if I can't forget the past and learn to believe you, to trust you? What then?'

'You don't have to forget the past.' He touched her face gently, his fingers moving over her cheek, her jaw and the silky skin of her throat. 'You just have to conquer it, and we can do that together. That is your first lesson in trust, my love, to believe me when you can't believe yourself. There is such a thing as happy ever after, but you have to reach out for it.'

'You'll get tired of waiting for me.'

'Never.' He smiled his beautiful smile that made her heart melt.

'There are hundreds of lovely women out there,' Sophy said a trifle desperately. 'Women without any hang-ups, women who would fall into your arms if you so much as clicked your fingers.'

'No, there is only you.' He took her face in his hands, his eyes stroking her. 'For me, that is.' And then he grinned as he added, 'But I appreciate your faith in my prowess.'

She smiled reluctantly. 'This isn't funny, Andreas.'

'No, it is not,' he agreed, his eyes suddenly serious. 'I have discovered that for myself. You are such a fragile-looking, delicate little thing, but you have this incredible will which I never guessed at when I first saw you. I thought it would be easy. I would wine you and dine you and you would fall madly in love with me, and that would be that.'

'I did fall madly in love with you.'

'But that was only the beginning of my fight to win you.'

He saw her eyes darken as he spoke and felt the slight withdrawal of the slender body in his arms. 'What is it?' he said quickly. 'What have I just said?'

'Nothing.' She dropped her eyes from his, her face tense.

'No, none of that,' he said grimly. 'From now on you speak from the heart, whether I will like it or not, and I shall do the same. No secrets, no fencing, no pretence.'

She was such a mess inside, she thought helplessly. He would get fed up with her—he would. And then, when she saw he wasn't about to give in, she murmured, 'I have always thought the reason my father married my mother in the first place was because she represented something of a challenge to him. He was used to women adoring him, and she did, she certainly did, but she held out for marriage before she would sleep with him. He had met someone who didn't fall into his arms so readily as all the others, and that was why he wanted her. Once they were married and Jill and I were on the way…'

'Sophy, I cannot deny that there are men like your father,' Andreas said quietly, 'only that I am not one of them. But words are cheap and words will not provide the balm you need on what is still an open wound. If you were pregnant with my child—' he paused for an infinitesimal second and she felt his hands tighten on her waist '—I would be the proudest man on earth. I would want to wrap you up in cotton wool and be with you every minute to protect you and our child. That is the natural response of a normal man. Your father—' He stopped abruptly, and shook his head, swearing softly in his own language.

'But we only met a couple of weeks ago,' Sophy pointed out with undeniable logic. 'How could we know if we're compatible?'

His eyes answered that question and she blushed hotly. He bent down, kissing her long and hard again, for good measure.

'Okay, so we're compatible,' she murmured when she'd got her breath back. 'But—'

'I will deal with the buts.' He moulded her against the hot, hard length of him. 'Or my name is not Andreas Karydis.'

'I have to go.' His self-assurance was frightening.

He understood instantly. 'That's not a problem,' he said with silky emphasis. 'Because I will see you at the weekend. I will see you at every weekend. Okay?'

'Andreas, this is crazy.' Her voice quavered a little in spite of all her efforts to project the cool, calm image that had protected her in the past. 'This whole thing is crazy.'

'Love is crazy, sweetheart.'

It was the second endearment since they had been talking and the quality of his voice sent her heart soaring before she called it to heel. 'We're only prolonging the agony,' she insisted with a brittle emphasis that told him she was near the end of her tether. 'I can't do this, any of it. I'm not what you think I am. I haven't got the energy to keep scraping at the wound, which is what you're asking; neither could I bury my head in the sand when it all began to go wrong.'

'It won't go wrong, so that deals with that one,' he said with magnificent determination. 'And it is not energy that is required, only courage, and you have that in abundance.'

She stared at him for long seconds, and then for the first

time since she had set eyes on Andreas Karydis the nagging sense of apprehension eased a little. 'You are so Greek,' she said weakly.

'But our children will have English blood too,' he responded with a devastating smile, 'so that is good, eh? But now you must check in for your flight, so we will return to the others, who will be very tactful and circumspect of course.' He grinned again.

'What are you going to say to them?' Sophy couldn't smile.

'The truth,' he answered simply. 'Just the truth.'

'Which is?' she asked nervously.

He stared at her, drinking in her fair, fragile beauty and the vulnerability in her face. 'That we are seeing each other,' he said quietly. 'That I love you with all my heart and intend to make you my wife, whatever it takes. That a moment spent apart from you is like a hundred years. That sort of thing.'

Their coffee was cold by the time they walked back into the terminal, but no one pointed it out. Evangelos took the news of their relationship completely in his stride and although Jill's eyes widened slightly she recovered quickly. It was left to Michael to say, with typical childish tactlessness, 'What does that mean? Seeing each other? Are you going to get married?'

'One day.' Andreas's voice was low and smoky.

'When?' Michael was all impatience, but in the next instant Jill had whisked him off his seat and carted him—not without protest—to wash his hands.

Sophy and Andreas were married ten months later, on a sunny Greek day when the sky was as blue as English cornflowers and the April sunshine was pleasantly warm.

They had both wanted the wedding to be in Halkidiki, and the little white church was full to bursting with English friends and relatives whom Andreas had flown over, along with a whole host of Greek ones. It was all colour and hushed excitement.

Michael was Andreas's best man—an honour which had the small boy as stiff and correct as a sergeant major—and Jill was Sophy's matron of honour and looked lovely in pale lemon. Christos had flown out with Sophy's sister and nephew; he had been a tower of strength for Jill since Theodore's death, and it was clear to anyone with eyes to see that the two had begun to think a great deal of each other.

But Sophy wasn't thinking about her sister's burgeoning romance; she had eyes for no one but her fiancé as she walked slowly down the aisle on Evangelos's arm. He looked stunningly handsome as he waited for her, Michael at the side of him as proud as punch. And the soft murmur of awe, as the assembled congregation turned and saw the bride, spoke of how beautiful Sophy looked in her ivory wedding dress of crushed silk, her lace veil as delicate as butterfly wings.

Andreas had spent nearly as much time in England as he had in Greece until he had persuaded Sophy to agree to marry him. She had said yes at Christmas, which she and Jill and Michael had spent in Greece with Evangelos and Dimitra, but she had known within days of arriving back in England in June that she couldn't live without him. He'd been right; he was in her head and her heart.

But the intervening time until Christmas had been necessary. The long-buried fears and issues which Andreas had brought to the surface had had to be faced and dealt with, and it had been hard. Very hard. She didn't think she could have got through without Andreas. But together they had faced the demons of fear, hurt, bitterness, resentment and not least doubt, and one by one the release had come and ghosts had been laid to rest.

'My darling. My precious, beautiful darling.'

As she reached Andreas's side his whisper was for her ears only, his eyes adoring her as she smiled up at him, happy and confident in his love.

She said her vows in a clear, soft voice that brought tears to Jill's eyes and made Dimitra reach for her handkerchief; Andreas's voice so ringing with pride that Evangelos remarked afterwards he was sure it could be heard ten miles away.

And then the service was over and they emerged from the church's flower-filled interior to a hail of rice and confetti, driving back to Evangelos's villa where a huge marquee had been erected in the grounds and a small army of caterers provided a banquet fit for royalty.

It was a wonderful day, a magical day, and the party went on long after the sky had turned to black velvet pierced with diamonds, the small band playing and the champagne still flowing into the early hours. No one wanted to go home!

But Andreas had stolen away with his bride long before then. They were spending their wedding night at home before flying to the Caribbean the next day for a month, and when at last Andreas carried her over the threshold they found Alethea had strewn rose petals over the floor to greet them. The delicate perfume filled the house, and on impulse Sophy pulled him into the garden where soft shadows danced in the moonlit fairyland.

It was still warm as they made their way down to the beach through the scented vegetation. The light was silvery, the full moon creating its own sense of whispering enchantment, and the sea sighed gently as it caressed the sand which shone white and gleaming. Everything was clean and newly washed.

'I thought we would never be alone.' Andreas's voice was dark and smoky and Sophy shivered in anticipation.

She had kicked off her wedding shoes in the house and taken off her veil and delicate gold and crystal headdress, and now she looked part of the night, her hair and billowy pale dress silvered by the ethereal light.

'You are so beautiful, exquisite,' he murmured softly as he took her fully into his arms. 'I'm almost afraid you will break if I hold you too close.'

'I won't break,' she assured him firmly. 'I want you to make love to me here, in the open with the sky and stars above us and the air as sweet as honey. And afterwards we will swim in the sea.' She smiled at him, the words a declaration.

'Skinny-dipping?' he asked teasingly, his eyes looking into hers. 'You are throwing off all your inhibitions for real, aren't you?'

'Oh, yes.' She stared at him with huge eyes, her face serious. 'This is a new beginning. My real life starts from now.'

He undressed her slowly, not least because the silk dress had endless tiny buttons, but then she stepped out of the dress and petticoats and watched his face as his eyes ran over her tantalising French underwear. The transparent cream lace bikini pants and suspender belt, and uplift bra which gave her a cleavage she'd never had before, had cost a small fortune but they were worth every penny. And she didn't feel shy, just overwhelmingly, fiercely in love as she watched the passion darken his face.

Andreas's hands were shaking slightly as he knelt down in front of her and unclipped first one suspender and then the other, peeling the silk, lace-topped stockings from her almost reverently.

As she stepped out of the last one he caught her ankle in his hands, kissing her foot with tiny burning kisses before he began to work upwards. She was shivering with desire by the time he removed the last of her clothing and, as he took her breasts in his hands, rubbing their peaks to throbbing sensitive life with his thumbs, she was already moist and ready for him.

She felt awe when Andreas was naked in front of her, hugely aroused, but in spite of his desire he touched and tasted her for a long time before he lay her on the blanket of their clothing. Sophy was in a feverish agony of need, no room in her mind for anything but her husband, and she welcomed him into her body with little cries that she was unaware of but which sent rippling contractions across Andreas's taut frame, as he tried to control his own passion until he had brought her to the peak of desire.

This was so different to anything she had known with Matthew that Sophy felt she had never been made love to before, but still Andreas delayed the moment of full release, pleasing her, and himself, until she felt her body wasn't able to contain the pleasure she was feeling and that it would shatter into a million pieces.

And then the wild rhythmic undulations that had been causing her to arch and twist hit the explosive trigger of his own need, and they disappeared over the edge together into a soaring world of pure undiluted sensation where nothing existed but each other.

His heart was beating like a hammer above hers when Sophy came back from that parallel universe, and he held her close, stroking her hair with loving fingers, kissing her face with quick burning caresses as he whispered endearments against her hot skin. It was all she could have hoped for and more.

'All I care about is you,' he murmured after a little while, 'you know that, don't you? You are everything I need, everything I will ever need. No other woman will ever touch my heart. I will love you for eternity.'

'I know,' she said softly, his body stirring again as she caressed him with hungry fingers. 'I know, my love.'

And she did. At last.

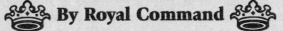

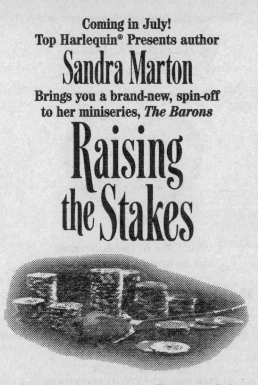

The world's bestselling romance series.

Seduction and Passion Guaranteed!

We're on the lookout for hot new authors...

Think you have what it takes to write a novel?

Then this is your chance!

These compelling modern fantasies capture the
drama and intensity of a powerful, sensual love
affair. The stories portray spirited, independent
heroines and irresistible heroes in international
settings. The conflict between these characters
should be balanced by a developing romance that
may include explicit lovemaking. Could you
transport readers into a world of provocative,
tantalizing romantic excitement?

[complete manuscript = 55,000 words]

Submissions to:
Harlequin Mills & Boon Editorial Department
Eton House, 18-24 Paradise Road, Richmond, Surrey
TW9 1SR, United Kingdom

If you enjoyed what you just read,
then we've got an offer you can't resist!

Take 2 bestselling
love stories FREE!

Plus get a FREE surprise gift!

The world's bestselling romance series.

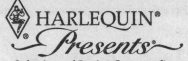

HARLEQUIN®
Presents

Seduction and Passion Guaranteed!

A new trilogy by **Carole Mortimer**

BACHELOR COUSINS

Three cousins of Scottish descent...they're male, millionaires and marriageable!

Meet Logan, Fergus and Brice, three tall, dark, handsome men about town. They've made their millions in London, but their hearts belong to the heather-clad hills of their grandfather McDonald's Scottish estate.

Logan, Fergus and Brice are about to give up their keenly fought-for bachelor status for three wonderful women—laugh, cry and read all about their trials and tribulations in their pursuit of love.

Coming next month:
To Marry McKenzie, #2261

Look out for:
To Marry McCloud
On-sale August, #2267

To Marry McAllister
On-sale September, #2273

Pick up a Harlequin Presents novel and you will enter a world of spine-tingling passion and provocative, tantalizing romance!

HARLEQUIN®
Makes any time special ®

Available wherever Harlequin books are sold.

Visit us at www.eHarlequin.com

HPBACH